Tim flinched. "Sara, will you just give me a chance? I know I've hurt you in the past, but I'm different now, and—"

"Listen," Sara broke in, her voice a fierce whisper, "I don't want you to tell anybody about the reform school, understand? I told everyone at school that you were living with Dad in Connecticut, that you get good grades, and that you're a member of the track team. And you'd better go along with the story."

Tim's eyes flashed. "You want me to lie?"

"It wouldn't be the first time, would it?" Sara countered.

Tim placed his hands on the table as if to steady himself. He looked carefully at his sister, and then spoke. "Sara, I *need* to be straight with people about where I've been and what I've done."

"If you don't back up my story, I'll never forgive you!" Sara hissed.

"I have a feeling you'll never forgive me anyway," Tim replied sadly.

Bantam Books in the Sweet Valley High series
Ask your bookseller for the books you have missed

#1 DOUBLE LOVE
#2 SECRETS
#3 PLAYING WITH FIRE
#4 POWER PLAY
#5 ALL NIGHT LONG
#6 DANGEROUS LOVE
#7 DEAR SISTER
#8 HEARTBREAKER
#9 RACING HEARTS
#10 WRONG KIND OF GIRL
#11 TOO GOOD TO BE TRUE
#12 WHEN LOVE DIES
#13 KIDNAPPED!
#14 DECEPTIONS
#15 PROMISES
#16 RAGS TO RICHES
#17 LOVE LETTERS
#18 HEAD OVER HEELS
#19 SHOWDOWN
#20 CRASH LANDING!
#21 RUNAWAY
#22 TOO MUCH IN LOVE
#23 SAY GOODBYE
#24 MEMORIES
#25 NOWHERE TO RUN
#26 HOSTAGE!
#27 LOVESTRUCK
#28 ALONE IN THE CROWD
#29 BITTER RIVALS
#30 JEALOUS LIES
#31 TAKING SIDES
#32 THE NEW JESSICA
#33 STARTING OVER
#34 FORBIDDEN LOVE
#35 OUT OF CONTROL
#36 LAST CHANCE
#37 RUMORS
#38 LEAVING HOME
#39 SECRET ADMIRER
#40 ON THE EDGE
#41 OUTCAST
#42 CAUGHT IN THE MIDDLE
#43 HARD CHOICES
#44 PRETENSES
#45 FAMILY SECRETS
#46 DECISIONS
#47 TROUBLEMAKER
#48 SLAM BOOK FEVER
#49 PLAYING FOR KEEPS
#50 OUT OF REACH
#51 AGAINST THE ODDS
#52 WHITE LIES
#53 SECOND CHANCE
#54 TWO-BOY WEEKEND
#55 PERFECT SHOT
#56 LOST AT SEA
#57 TEACHER CRUSH
#58 BROKENHEARTED
#59 IN LOVE AGAIN
#60 THAT FATAL NIGHT
#61 BOY TROUBLE
#62 WHO'S WHO?
#63 THE NEW ELIZABETH
#64 THE GHOST OF TRICIA MARTIN
#65 TROUBLE AT HOME
#66 WHO'S TO BLAME?
#67 THE PARENT PLOT
#68 THE LOVE BET
#69 FRIEND AGAINST FRIEND
#70 MS. QUARTERBACK
#71 STARRING JESSICA!
#72 ROCK STAR'S GIRL
#73 REGINA'S LEGACY
#74 THE PERFECT GIRL
#75 AMY'S TRUE LOVE
#76 MISS TEEN SWEET VALLEY
#77 CHEATING TO WIN
#78 THE DATING GAME
#79 THE LONG-LOST BROTHER

Super Editions: PERFECT SUMMER
SPECIAL CHRISTMAS
SPRING BREAK
MALIBU SUMMER
WINTER CARNIVAL
SPRING FEVER

Super Thrillers: DOUBLE JEOPARDY
ON THE RUN
NO PLACE TO HIDE
DEADLY SUMMER

Super Stars: LILA'S STORY
BRUCE'S STORY
ENID'S STORY

Magna Edition: THE WAKEFIELDS OF SWEET VALLEY

THE LONG-LOST BROTHER

Written by
Kate William

Created by
FRANCINE PASCAL

BANTAM BOOKS
NEW YORK • TORONTO • LONDON • SYDNEY • AUCKLAND

RL 6, age 12 and up

THE LONG-LOST BROTHER
A Bantam Book / October 1991

Conceived by Francine Pascal

Produced by Daniel Weiss Associates, Inc.
33 West 17th Street
New York, NY 10011

Cover art by James Mathewuse

ISBN 0-553-29214-5

Published simultaneously in the United States and Canada

Bantam Books are published by Bantam Books, a division of Bantam Doubleday Dell Publishing Group, Inc. Its trademark, consisting of the words "Bantam Books" and the portrayal of a rooster, is Registered in U.S. Patent and Trademark Office and in other countries. Marca Registrada. Bantam Books, 666 Fifth Avenue, New York, New York 10103.

PRINTED IN THE UNITED STATES OF AMERICA

OPM 0 9 8 7 6 5 4 3 2 1

To Sarah Hohenwarter

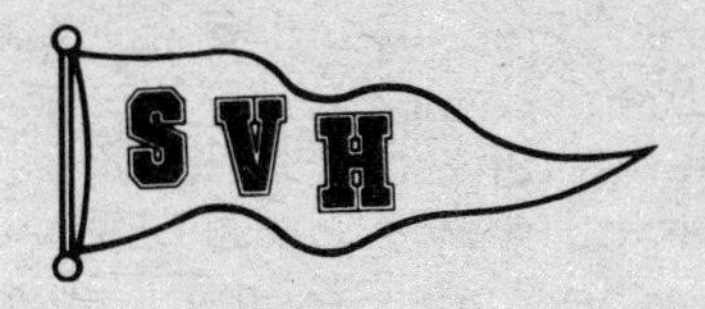

One

Sixteen-year-old Elizabeth Wakefield, a junior at Sweet Valley High, tapped the eraser end of her pencil against her chin. Her sun-streaked blond hair was pulled back into an attractive French braid and her skin was tanned to a golden glow. Her new white jeans and blue tank top showed off her perfect size-six figure.

At the moment, though, the last thing Elizabeth was thinking about was her looks. A thoughtful expression shone in her aquamarine eyes. Her mind was spinning as she tried to absorb all the things she had learned in this interview for *The Oracle,* Sweet Valley High's newspaper.

Mrs. Marstowe, head of the local shelter for battered women, sat across from her, behind a cluttered desk. "So you see, Elizabeth, abused women come from all economic and educational backgrounds. Quite a lot are married to professional people—doctors, lawyers, teachers, even clergymen—and many are also professionals themselves."

Elizabeth's forehead crinkled in a frown. "I can understand why some women would stay with men who abuse them. I mean, women with little money or education or self-esteem, or no family or friends to help them make a new start. But I really can't figure out why the others don't just pack their bags and leave."

The social worker smiled patiently. "There is no simple explanation, Elizabeth. But the primary reason is that too many women have little or no confidence in their own ability to make lives for themselves without the help and support of a man."

"When the women come here to you, how do you help them?" The whole problem seemed overwhelming to Elizabeth. "Where do you *start?*"

Mrs. Marstowe traced the handle of her coffee mug with the tip of one finger while she considered her answer. Finally she said, "We begin with counseling both individually and in groups. If the situation at home is dangerous, and it almost always is, we bring the women and their children to the shelter, which isn't far from here, to live until something more permanent can be worked out."

Elizabeth wrote busily in her notebook. She was familiar with the community center itself;

she had done an article on Project Youth, a clinic based at the center. Her twin sister Jessica's friend, Amy Sutton, and Amy's boyfriend, Barry Rork, were active volunteers on the hotline for troubled teens.

"Where is the shelter?" Elizabeth asked.

"That's a secret," Mrs. Marstowe answered quietly.

"Of course," Elizabeth said. "In order to protect your clients, you would have to have a safe place for them to hide." She shifted in her chair. "How do women in trouble find the shelter?"

"The police often bring them to us after there's been a 'domestic disturbance,' as they call it. And we can always be reached by telephone. Our number is listed in the white pages, and it's widely publicized. Sometimes our volunteers and counselors go and pick the women up, after they've asked for help, of course."

"What happens when the women arrive at the shelter?"

Mrs. Marstowe turned in her swivel chair to fill her cup from the pot of coffee on the credenza behind her desk. "We see that any medical needs are taken care of first, naturally. After that, it's largely a matter of providing food, warmth, clothing, and counseling until other arrangements can be made. Ideally, the client continues to visit a counselor for some time after she goes out on her own."

Elizabeth brightened. "Most of the women

do succeed at making new lives for themselves, then?"

Mrs. Marstowe shook her head regretfully. "Unfortunately, quite the opposite is true. The majority return to their troubled home situations and the problem gets progressively worse." She smiled wisely at Elizabeth's disappointed expression. "But we are making progress, Elizabeth. We are getting the word out that violent behavior is not OK, that there are places to go and people who want to help."

Elizabeth nodded and closed her notebook. "Could I visit the shelter itself one day soon?"

The older woman considered the request for a moment, then replied, "I don't see why not. The problem of domestic violence needs all the publicity it can get. You understand, of course, that the actual whereabouts of the shelter must be kept completely confidential."

Elizabeth promised to keep the location a secret. She thanked Mrs. Marstowe, and said goodbye.

Typical California weather greeted her when she left the building. The day was bright and warm. Jessica was waiting at the curb, as she had promised, in the red Fiat Spider the twins shared. Jessica was revving the engine and there was a grim expression on her face.

Jessica had a tan the color of warm honey, too, along with a terrific size-six figure and beautiful blue-green eyes. Her hair was exactly the same shade of blond as Elizabeth's, but no style as tame as a French braid would do for Jessica's hair. It fell freely around her shoulders, glistening and sexy. And when it came to personalities, the twins were as different as their hairstyles. Elizabeth was the more thoughtful of the two. She enjoyed reading good books, writing for *The Oracle,* and spending time with her boyfriend, Todd Wilkins. Jessica, on the other hand, was the more impulsive one. Her life was almost totally dedicated to shopping, boys, and cheerleading. But in spite of their differences, the twins were best friends.

"It's about time," Jessica snapped as Elizabeth opened the passenger door and got into the car. "This may come as a big shock to you, Liz, but I have other things to do besides play chauffeur to my sister!"

Elizabeth was almost grateful for Jessica's irritable mood; it provided a welcome distraction from the heavy subject she had been dealing with all that afternoon. "Like what?" she asked.

It was clear that Jessica's legendary temper was sizzling, but Elizabeth was glad her sister didn't allow it to make her a reckless driver as she steered the Fiat out into the light afternoon traffic. Only recently, Mr. and Mrs. Wakefield had made a point of repeating their law regarding the twins' use of the small red car. If either of them was careless behind the wheel, she would have to hand over her keys and walk until further notice.

"It's Friday," Jessica pointed out. "I have a date with Steve Anderson. We're going to a beach party and I have exactly half an hour to get ready!"

Elizabeth let out a long breath, and her soft blond bangs danced against her forehead. It *was* Jessica's turn to have the car, and coming to pick up her twin had probably been an inconvenience.

"I'm sorry, Jess," Elizabeth said quietly. "I really appreciate it."

Jessica downshifted for a stoplight. While they waited for it to turn green, she snatched up her sunglasses from the dashboard and put them on. "What were you doing at the community center, anyway? Didn't you already write an article about that Project Kids Clinic, or whatever it is?"

Elizabeth couldn't help but smile, despite her gloomy thoughts. "Project Youth," she corrected. "This time I'm doing a piece on battered women."

The light changed and Jessica pressed her foot down on the gas pedal, sending the little car zooming through the intersection. "You mean women whose husbands *hit them?*"

"Yes," Elizabeth answered sadly.

Expertly, Jessica rummaged through her bag, keeping her eyes on the road the whole time, and brought out a stick of gum. After unwrapping it, she folded it into her mouth.

"Bummer," she said, consulting the rearview mirror before signaling and changing lanes.

* * *

A pile of letters and magazines lay on the small hooked rug just inside the front door. Sara Eastborne bent to gather them up with a graceful sweep of one hand and set them aside on the hall table. She wished her mom would get a regular mailbox instead of that old-fashioned slot in the door.

"Aren't you even going to look and see if you got any mail?" Sara's best friend, Amanda Hayes, asked. Amanda, like Sara, was a junior at Sweet Valley High, and the pair had a lot in common. Both were popular and got good grades, and both excelled in modern dance.

Sara picked up the stack again and flipped through the envelopes, mostly for show. There was a thin envelope from her father, addressed to her mother—*probably just the monthly support check,* she thought, since he never bothered to write—a bill, a sales flier, another bill.

And a letter from Tim.

Sara's stomach jumped nervously. She shuffled the plump envelope back in with the other mail and tossed it all nonchalantly onto the coffee table as she passed through the living room.

"Nothing for me," she said with an airy sigh, but her emotions were churning. She wished she could forget that her twin brother, Tim, even existed. Telling her best friend and the other kids at Sweet Valley High the truth about him was out of the question.

Sara led the way into the kitchen, where she set down her books and her dance bag and went over to the refrigerator. Her face, reflected back to her between the magnets and notes stuck to the shiny metal door, looked troubled. She tossed her shoulder-length dark hair back, opened the door, and took out two sodas, setting them on the counter.

"How do you think you did on the French quiz?" she asked, not quite meeting Amanda's intelligent hazel eyes. Sara's hand trembled a little as she filled two tall glasses with ice, and then poured the fizzing soda over the ice.

"I aced it, just like you did," Amanda answered, without a trace of conceit. When Sara turned to look at her friend, she saw that Amanda was frowning.

"What's bothering you?" Amanda asked as she flipped her long auburn hair over her shoulder. "You were in a great mood until you looked through the mail."

So many times Sara had wanted to tell Amanda all about Tim and the terrible trouble he had gotten himself into, but she had never been able to bring herself to take the risk. Amanda, Bob Hillman, who was Sara's boyfriend, and the other kids at Sweet Valley High all meant too much to her. She couldn't take a chance on losing their friendship and respect because of Tim. She *wouldn't* pay for his mistakes.

Knowing Amanda wouldn't let the subject

drop without some kind of explanation, Sara decided to tell a partial lie. "I saw that we got a check from my dad, that's all. You know, he never asks how we are, how I'm doing in school, or whether I've made friends since Mom and I moved to Sweet Valley. I wish that, just once, he'd care enough to ask a few questions, instead of just signing the support check and having his secretary mail it off."

Amanda's parents, Bill and Sharon Hayes, were happily married, but Sara saw sympathy and understanding in her friend's face all the same. And it made Sara feel ashamed for altering the truth the way she had.

"That must be hard," Amanda said, nodding her thanks when Sara handed her a glass of soda. "Maybe if you wrote to your dad, or called him on the phone . . ."

Sara had to look away for a moment so that her friend wouldn't see the lie in her eyes. Sure, it hurt that her father showed so little interest in her, but he had been like that even before the divorce. She was used to it. "It's OK," she said quietly. "I don't need him any more than he needs me."

Amanda took a sip of her soda. "Tell me about your brother," she said after a moment.

Sara flinched. Again, she turned away and busied herself searching the cupboards for chips. With her back to her friend, she managed an offhanded shrug. "What's to tell?" she said, hoping there wasn't a tremor in her voice. "He and I are twins—fraternal, of course. After the divorce, Tim decided to stay in Connecticut with my dad."

"Do you miss him?"

Yes, answered a voice deep within Sara's heart, but she shook her head and said, "Not really. We never had much in common."

"Except the same birthday and the same parents."

Sara found the chips, pulled them from the shelf, and closed the cupboard door with slightly more force than necessary. "Can we talk about something else, please?"

When Sara finally dared to meet Amanda's eyes again, she could tell that she had hurt her friend's feelings. "I'm sorry," Sara said truthfully. She sighed. "I shouldn't have snapped at you like that. I . . . I guess I'm still not over my parents' divorce, and how Tim and I ended up apart."

"Whenever you're ready to talk, you know you can come to me," Amanda answered, and Sara thought how lucky she was to have such a terrific friend, and how terrible it would be to lose her. Unfortunately, it wasn't hard to imagine losing Amanda. Sara had lost other friends, back in Connecticut—because of Tim.

When Sara's mother, Janet Eastborne, came home from work later that afternoon, she was carrying a roll of blueprints under one arm.

Sara thought that she looked particularly tired. Mrs. Eastborne was an architect with a prominent local firm, and a friend and colleague of Elizabeth and Jessica's mother. She gave Sara a thankful, but weary smile when she saw that dinner was almost ready.

"What would I do without you?" Mrs. Eastborne asked, sinking into a chair at the kitchen table. On her way to the kitchen she had picked up the day's mail.

Sara poured a cup of coffee for her mother and set it down on the tabletop. She didn't miss the eager way Mrs. Eastborne opened the envelope from Tim.

"He's been taking a special class in car repair, through the vocational high school," Mrs. Eastborne said. Sara thought her mother made it sound as if Tim had mastered neurosurgery or something. "You know how he loves cars."

"That must be why he stole one," Sara muttered on her way to the refrigerator for the green salad she had prepared earlier.

Mrs. Eastborne's eyes raced across the lines of the letter, her smile growing warmer and more genuine as she read. "What did you say, sweetheart?" she asked pleasantly.

"Nothing," Sara lied, setting the salad bowl on the table with an audible thump.

Janet Eastborne sighed and set the letter aside. "I really miss Tim."

No kidding, Sara thought sourly. Nothing in the world would have made her admit that she missed Tim sometimes, too—that *other* Tim, the one she hadn't seen since before all the trouble started. "I have a dinner date with Bob tonight, so I won't be eating with you," she said aloud, as if her twin's name hadn't been mentioned. "I might be out late."

Mrs. Eastborne sighed. "Sara, we need to talk."

"About Tim?" Sara's voice was brittle. She pretended to be absorbed in the process of setting the table. "What is there to say, Mom? He's an embarrassment to the whole family. He drank too much, he took drugs, and finally he stole a car. Now he's in reform school. Doesn't that about cover it?"

"No, it doesn't," Mrs. Eastborne replied firmly. "Sara, Tim made some terrible mistakes. There's no denying that. But he's really trying to turn his life around now. He's been getting good grades at school and attending Alcoholics Anonymous meetings."

Sara was trembling with the effort to hold in all her anger and pain. "And that makes everything all right?" she finally cried, her eyes filling with tears. "Mom, have you forgotten how good Tim was at faking us all out? Making us think he was this wonderful guy, when all the time . . ."

Mrs. Eastborne stood and took her daughter gently but firmly by the shoulders. "Sweetheart, I'm not saying we have to pretend we weren't hurt and humiliated by some of the things Tim did. But he's part of this family. I think he deserves a second chance!"

Angrily, Sara wiped away her tears with the back of her hand. *"This family?"* she cried. "*What* family, Mom? Maybe we had a family once, but Tim ruined it, just as he ruined everything else!"

"Sara—"

Sara pulled away from her mother, refusing to listen. She ran into her room, slammed the door behind her, and flung herself onto her bed. She reached for the stuffed toy cat her father had brought back for her a long time ago when he had come home from a business trip.

There was a soft knock at the door, and then Mrs. Eastborne came in without waiting for an invitation. She sat on the edge of Sara's bed and laid one hand on her daughter's back.

"Sara, you can't run away from your feelings. You need to work them through, and I think the best way for you to do that would be to start going to Alateen. There's a meeting tonight at the community center."

Sara knew that Alateen was a self-help group, adapted from Alcoholics Anonymous, for kids with an alcoholic friend or relative. She was definitely in no mood to go to a meeting and sit around listening to other people's problems. Her own were swamping her as it was.

"I'll be all right," she said stonily.

"You know that I practice what I preach," Mrs. Eastborne persisted quietly. "I've been going to Al-Anon meetings. And Sara, what I learned there is that alcoholism is a family disease. It's affected all of us, not just Tim."

Sara sniffled. It was true that her mother seemed happier and more peaceful since she had started going to Al-Anon, the adult version of Alateen. But Sara was sure that she personally didn't need help. Everything would be all right if only Tim would change. "I guess I'd better get ready for my date with Bob," she said after a long time.

Mrs. Eastborne was discouraged, Sara could feel it, but she didn't say anything else. She just patted Sara's shoulder lightly and left the room.

Sara's slate-gray eyes had always been her best feature, contrasting beautifully with her dark hair, but that night when her boyfriend picked her up for their date, her lids were puffy and red from crying.

"You OK?" Bob asked, holding open the door of his father's shiny red BMW and frowning as Sara slid into the passenger seat.

Sara drew a deep breath and busily fastened her seat belt. "Nothing being an only child wouldn't cure," she murmured, but only after Bob had started to walk around the car and she could be sure he wouldn't hear. "I'm fine," she fibbed brightly when Bob was settled in the driver's seat.

Bob's green eyes gazed curiously at Sara for a moment before he started the engine. A second later, he pushed back his thick blond hair and grinned his famous grin, setting Sara's heart to beating faster and making her stomach pitch as if she had just stepped onto some wild carnival ride.

"You look sensational tonight," he said with an approving glance at Sara's pale yellow dress. "Mom and Dad will be impressed."

Though she had been looking forward to the evening for weeks, Sara suddenly felt a little uncomfortable at the prospect of meeting Bob's parents *and* dining at the Sweet Valley Country Club. She wished she could just run back home and make peace with her mother, find some way to smooth over the rough spots between them.

"Thanks," she said softly.

Tiny lights twinkled in the branches of the trees on the far side of the swimming pool, their reflections dancing on the dark turquoise water. The whole scene reminded Sara of the good old days, back in Connecticut, when her mother and father had still been married and Tim had still been behaving like a normal teenager. They had had a membership in a club like this one, and in those years Sara had felt as if she really belonged.

A painful twinge of homesickness struck

Sara, and she stepped a little closer to Bob. Once she had been a part of the elite crowd, but now—well, now she might as well have been a gate-crasher, for all the self-confidence she had. She almost expected someone to rush up to her and demand to see proof that she was important enough to be there.

She imagined how it would feel if all the other guests knew that she was the sister of an alcoholic and a drug addict who was in the habit of stealing cars. She pictured everyone present stopping their conversation to turn and stare at her.

"Sara," Bob growled, his country-club smile never faltering, "you look like you're about to turn around and run for your life. Snap out of it, will you? I want my folks to see you at your best!"

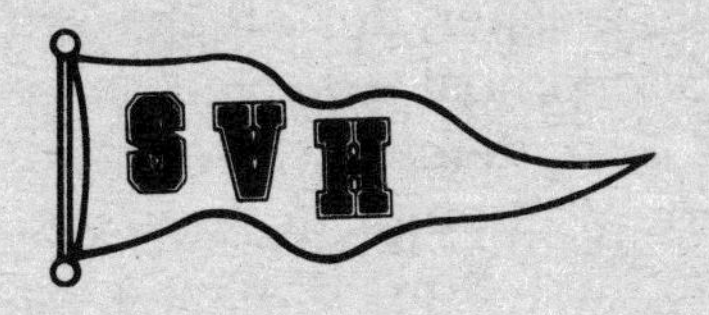

Two

Bob led Sara over to his parents' table near the pool. His father rose from his chair and nodded a greeting, but he seemed distracted, his gaze roaming beyond Sara and Bob as though they were invisible.

Bob pulled out Sara's chair for her. "Mom, Dad, I'd like you to meet Sara Eastborne. Sara, my parents, Mr. and Mrs. Hillman."

Sara smiled nervously. It was so important to please Bob and to make a good impression on his family. "Hello, Mr. and Mrs. Hillman," she said politely.

"Hello, Sara," Mrs. Hillman responded, her tone brittle, her smile stiff.

Mr. Hillman muttered some greeting, still searching the faces of the other party guests. Sara was painfully reminded of her own father, who always seemed to have better things to do than pay attention to his children or his wife.

"Your father is eager to talk with Tom Walsh about a new investment opportunity," Mrs. Hillman said, in an apparent effort to explain her husband's less-than-gracious manner.

Mr. Hillman must have spotted Mr. Walsh at that very moment. He suddenly bolted to his feet and rushed away from the table without explaining his sudden departure.

All through dinner, Mr. Hillman continued to leap out of his chair to talk with potential clients of his investment company. When he remained at the table, he talked of nothing but his expensive cars and the family's summer home on an island off the coast of Washington state. Mrs. Hillman spoke incessantly of the high price of hiring a decorator and the importance of projecting what she called "a suitable image."

Sara grew more uncomfortable with every passing moment. Bob's attitude and his parents' talk made her feel like a life-sized paper doll instead of a person.

After a while, as the superficial chatter continued around her, Sara found herself thinking of Tim and the good times they had had together before he started getting into trouble on such a regular basis. She remembered sledding down the steep hill behind their house during snowy Connecticut winters, and video-game competitions in front of the TV in the family room. In those days, she and Tim had communicated on a level that no one else had been able to share or understand. Being not only brother and sister, but *twins,* had created a deep and special bond between them.

"Sara?" Once again, Bob's voice was thick with disapproval. "My mother asked what you think about the controversy over tanning salons."

Startled, Sara stared at Mrs. Hillman and struggled to gather her scattered thoughts. In truth, she felt that doctors were right to be concerned about the dangers of long-term tanning. But looking at Bob's mother, with her California-golden skin, her artfully plucked eyebrows, and her perfectly made-up eyes, Sara couldn't bring herself to say what she truly believed.

"I haven't really thought about it," she said. The moment the words left her lips she felt stupid. Why couldn't she have come across with a more polished response? Bob was going to think she was nothing but an airhead!

Mrs. Hillman stabbed a piece of fresh crabmeat with her fork and frowned, letting Sara know exactly what she thought of dinner guests who didn't pay attention to their hosts.

"You really blew it with Mom and Dad," Bob muttered as he wrenched open the passenger door of his car for Sara.

For a moment Sara was furious. Then she remembered how much she liked Bob Hillman, and how popular he was at school. She sighed and, after he was behind the wheel again, reached out to touch his arm lightly.

"I'm sorry," she said. "I didn't mean to be rude. It's just that I have some things on my mind."

Bob's jaw was set tight as he turned the key in the ignition, but when he turned to look at Sara directly again, his expression softened. "What things?" he asked.

Sara bit her lip. *What things?* she thought miserably. *Just a lawbreaking brother who'll probably have his picture hanging in the post office by the time he's twenty. And it won't be because he's President.*

"Just some stuff between my mom and me," she said finally. It gave her a lonely feeling, not being able to tell either Bob or Amanda the truth about Tim. Her mother had been right about one thing—talking about her problems openly probably would make her feel better. But there was no one she felt comfortable talking *with.*

Bob's mood seemed to brighten a little as they pulled out into traffic. "Lila Fowler's throwing a party at the beach tomorrow. Want to go?"

Sara was relieved that Bob still wanted to date her, and she knew the party would be fun, even though Lila Fowler, the daughter of a very wealthy man, wasn't one of her favorite people.

"OK, sure," she answered. "I'd like that."

Bob grinned. "Wear that white swimsuit you bought last week, OK?" he said. "I want all the other guys to wish you were *their* girlfriend."

Sara felt vaguely uncomfortable, but she ignored the sensation. Bob just wanted her to look her best, she figured. There was nothing wrong with that.

On Saturday morning, Sara was awakened by the shrill ring of the telephone. Hoping for a call from Bob, or maybe Amanda, she sat up in bed and grabbed the receiver off the nightstand. Before she could say a word, however, she realized that her mother had already picked up the call in another room.

"Hello?"

"Hi, Mom." The voice was deeper than Sara remembered. "It's Tim. How are you?"

Sara felt sudden, inexplicable tears burn in her eyes. She wanted to say hello to Tim, maybe even ask how he had been doing, but her anger was much greater than this one small impulse toward peace.

"I'm fine, darling," Mrs. Eastborne answered, her tone warm with delight. "Gosh, it's really good to hear your voice."

Hang up, Sara thought, frustrated with herself. *Hang up!*

But she couldn't do it, not yet. As furious as Sara was with her twin brother, something inside her needed a moment of closeness with Tim, even if it was accidental and he didn't have the faintest idea she was there.

Suddenly Sara was startled out of her moment

of reflection, realizing that she had missed something Tim had said.

"Have you seen your dad lately?" Mrs. Eastborne asked.

"He visited last Sunday," Tim answered. Though the reply was positive, Sara sensed a layer of loneliness and hurt beneath her brother's words.

She didn't want to hear about Tim's pain, and she knew without being told that their dad had probably stopped in at the reform school for a few minutes, given Tim an expensive present, and left again.

Sara replaced the receiver as gently as she could, hoping Tim and Mrs. Eastborne wouldn't realize she had been listening, and got out of bed. She took a long time showering, styling, and blow-drying her hair, and by the time she went into the kitchen, wearing the white swimsuit Bob liked under her best pink shorts and top, her mother had already gone.

There was a note stuck on the refrigerator door.

Sweetheart,

I'm putting in some overtime at the office today. If there's anything you need, you can reach me there.

See you at dinner.

Love, Mom

Sara was glad her mother had already gone. Now she wouldn't have to hear all the latest about Tim. But strangely, standing alone in the kitchen, she felt a little abandoned.

Sara took a container of yogurt from the refrigerator and an apple from the fruit bowl and sat down in the kitchen to eat. Her eyes kept straying to the white wall phone next to the sink, and she was surprised to realize that she knew Tim's number at the school by heart. It was odd, she thought, her knowing the number, because she had no intention of calling him, now or ever.

The ring of the telephone made her jump for the second time that morning, and it was only with the greatest reluctance that she answered. It could be Tim calling back for some reason, and she had absolutely nothing to say to him. Nothing and everything.

It was Amanda's voice that chimed happily in her ear, though. "Hi. Did you have fun at the country club last night?"

"Of course. It was lovely," she lied.

Amanda laughed. "You're a better woman than I am! The country club has more snobs per square inch than any other place in Sweet Valley. A little rich for my blood," she answered.

There was a short, difficult silence, then Amanda turned the conversation in another direction. "I called because there's a huge sale at the mall today, and I thought you might like to go and hang out."

Sara's first impulse was to say an enthusiastic

yes, but then she remembered her date with Bob to attend Lila Fowler's beach party. "What time did you want to go?" Sara asked, even though she already knew the two events would conflict. *I'm getting entirely too good at faking feelings,* she thought uncomfortably.

"About one o'clock," Amanda answered, and Sara noted that her friend's tone was a little stiff. *She probably already senses that I mean to refuse,* Sara thought. "I can't," she said, closing her eyes for a moment. "Bob and I have plans for the afternoon."

"Why didn't you just say that in the first place?" Amanda asked.

"I guess I was hoping I could do both," Sara finally said. "Weren't you invited to Lila's party?"

"Yes." Amanda paused. "She invited the entire junior class and most of the senior class. I can only take Lila and her crowd in small doses, though. Some of those people are so superficial and phony."

Although Sara knew her friend's criticism wasn't directed at her personally, it still stung a little. Though she wanted Amanda's approval desperately, she wanted Bob's even more. "OK, well, I'll call you tonight."

"OK," Amanda replied, without much enthusiasm.

Sara said goodbye and hung up. She hadn't gotten two steps from the telephone before it rang again.

"Eastborne residence," she said.

Her father's deep voice replied, "Hello, kitten. How are you?"

Sara swallowed. So many times she had hoped her dad would call, and now that he had, she didn't know what to say to him. "I'm—I'm fine."

"That's good," Mr. Eastborne answered. "How's school?"

"I like Sweet Valley High a lot," Sara answered cheerfully, pretending, as he was, that things were OK between the two of them. "My classes and teachers are great, and I really like the kids."

"Terrific." Her father paused to clear his throat. "Listen, kitten, is your mother around?"

"She's at the office." Sara swallowed hard in an effort to control her emotions. "I can give you the number there."

"I have it, thanks," Mr. Eastborne said, and he sounded distracted now, impatient to get on with his business. "You're sure everything's all right out there?"

Sara's eyes were burning with tears she couldn't explain, but she made her voice sound bright. "Just sensational, Dad."

"Good," Mr. Eastborne replied. "Well, I guess I'll go ahead and call your mother. You take care of yourself."

"You, too," Sara chimed back happily, but when she hung up, her cheeks were streaked with tears.

* * *

Jessica was wearing a pink formal, her crown, and her Miss Teen Sweet Valley sash that morning as she stood at the kitchen counter spreading jam on an English muffin. Elizabeth couldn't help but giggle when she walked in.

Jessica narrowed her beautiful aquamarine eyes. "What's so funny?" she demanded.

Elizabeth disguised a chuckle as a cough. "Nothing," she answered. "Nothing at all. Cutting the ribbon at another car wash this morning?"

"Ugh," Jessica grumbled. "This time it's the new bowling alley. My whole Saturday is totally shot. It'll be almost two o'clock before I get through posing for pictures with Mayor Santelli."

Elizabeth grinned as she poured a glass of milk to go with the apple and croissant she was having for breakfast. "You wanted this, remember, Jess? You worked very hard to win the Miss Teen Sweet Valley title."

Jessica popped the last piece of muffin into her mouth and wiped her hands carefully on a paper towel. When she turned back to her sister, the full skirts of her formal rustled. She narrowed her eyes again, this time in obvious speculation. "I was just thinking of how you filled in for me the night of the pageant, during the swimsuit competition. . . ."

Elizabeth raised both hands and shook her head. "No way, Jess," she said. "*You're* Miss

Teen Sweet Valley, and I'm not going to put on your sash and crown and pretend to be you so you can get to Lila's beach party on time."

Jessica pretended to be hurt and said poutingly, "How could you think that I would *do* that to you?" Then she arched her eyebrows and asked, "Are you helping Dad clean the garage today or something?"

"No. Steven's home for the weekend, remember?" Elizabeth answered. "He and Dad are going to do a little male bonding by stacking boxes and sorting junk together."

"Well, if you're not helping Dad, what are you doing in that grubby old outfit?"

Elizabeth looked down at her jeans and T-shirt before replying. "Mrs. Marstowe—she's one of the staff at the community center—is taking Enid and me to the battered women's shelter."

Jessica rolled her eyes. "Why would you want to do something so *depressing* when you could go to Lila's party or, better yet, pass yourself off as Miss Teen Sweet Valley?"

"Go figure," Elizabeth said, with a teasing smile.

"Did I hear something about a battered women's shelter?" Mrs. Wakefield asked as she entered the kitchen, looking trim and attractive in her white tennis outfit.

"Lady Bountiful here is going to pass out fruit or something," Jessica answered as she carefully smoothed her billowing skirts.

Mrs. Wakefield turned her attention to Elizabeth. "I take it you're writing an article for *The Oracle*."

Elizabeth nodded. "It's sad to think of violence happening in a family. Home should be a safe place."

Alice Wakefield rested her hand on Elizabeth's shoulder. "You may not believe it," she said gently, "but you're helping in your own way by writing responsible articles. As long as society ignores such problems, very little progress will be made. The more people are forced to *think* about domestic violence, to face the fact that it really is happening, the sooner we'll find lasting solutions."

Jessica sighed, glanced impatiently at the clock, and said, "On that inspirational note, I guess I'll head for the bowling alley."

When the door closed behind her sister, Elizabeth grinned. "Good thing we don't have to depend on Jess to turn the political and social tide."

Mrs. Wakefield laughed and held her tennis racquet aloft. "I'm meeting Janice Clemons for a match, and it's time I left. Since it's apparently still Jess's turn to drive the Fiat, would you like me to drop you off somewhere?"

Elizabeth shook her head. "Enid's picking me up, but thanks," she answered.

Mrs. Wakefield paused in the kitchen doorway and regarded her daughter with gentle affection. "I know you care a great deal about other people, Elizabeth, and I'm proud of you for that. But don't let the things you might see or hear about at the shelter get to you too much. None of us can change the world single-handedly."

"I'll remember," Elizabeth promised. "I guess I do tend to be a crusader sometimes."

Mrs. Wakefield smiled and left.

Ten minutes later Enid Rollins arrived. She, too, was dressed casually in jeans and a T-shirt, and she greeted her friend with an anxious grin.

"I'm kind of nervous," Enid confessed.

Elizabeth nodded. "So am I. Thanks for coming along to lend moral support."

Enid chuckled, putting the car into reverse and looking back over one shoulder as she eased out onto the street. "If it weren't for the things I do to 'lend moral support' to you, Liz, my life would be incredibly boring!"

Sara was not having a particularly good time at the beach party. It wasn't only the mysterious call from her father that troubled her, or the awkward conversation she had had earlier with Amanda. She just couldn't shake the feeling that something disastrous was about to happen.

Because she knew it was important to Bob that she appear to be having a good time, Sara threw herself into the volleyball tournament. Some of the other kids were surfing and some were swimming; others danced in the sand to the loud music of a rock band Lila's father had hired.

At about three o'clock in the afternoon Jessica Wakefield arrived and, as always, her appearance caused something of a stir. But Sara hardly noticed Jessica. She had too much on her mind even to feel jealous when the volleyball hit Bob in the head because he had been watching Jessica instead of paying attention to their game.

The music continued to flow, and so did the food and the fun. When the sun went down, some of the guys built a bonfire on the beach. Stars popped out overhead, some so big they looked like chips of ice.

It was late when the party finally broke up and Bob and Sara headed home. Bob had brought his car to a stop in Sara's driveway before she noticed he seemed annoyed again.

What have I done now? she wondered, a little irritated herself.

"If you didn't want to go to the party, you should have said so," Bob informed her grimly.

Sara was surprised. Until that moment, she had thought she'd done a good job of pretending she was having fun.

"You were a million miles away all day," Bob went on. "Sara, what's going on with you?"

Sara looked away. "It's just . . . maybe we could talk about it some other time."

"Yeah," Bob snapped as he shoved open his car door. "Right." He walked Sara to her front door and waited until she put her key in the lock before turning and walking away. He didn't kiss her goodnight and he didn't promise to call.

Sara was already feeling pretty down when she went into the house and found her mother waiting for her. Her mind flashed back to that morning's phone call from Mr. Eastborne.

"What is it?" she asked quickly.

Mrs. Eastborne drew a deep breath and let it out slowly. She looked unusually young standing there beside the fireplace in her jeans and lightweight sweatshirt. "It's Tim," she said. "They're releasing him from the reform school, and he's decided he'd like to come here to Sweet Valley to make a new start."

Sara sank into a chair, her knees suddenly too weak to support her. Her ears began to ring. "And you told him it would be all right?" she asked. "For him to come and live with us, I mean?"

Mrs. Eastborne raised her chin a notch. "Yes," she replied, and in that moment Sara felt as if the whole world had crashed down on top of her.

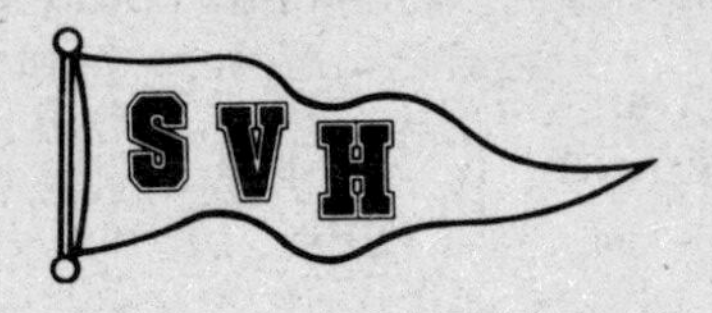

Three

On Sunday, Elizabeth sat at her desk, pen in hand, her journal open to the previous day's page. She wanted to write about her Saturday-morning visit to the battered women's shelter, but she couldn't seem to find the words.

She sighed and sat back in her chair, remembering.

The shelter was a big, old Victorian-style house, situated in one of Sweet Valley's quieter neighborhoods. There were no signs out front to identify it, and the mailbox at the side of the road was unmarked.

Elizabeth tapped the end of her pen against her chin. The Sanctuary, as it was called by those who lived and worked there, had in some ways been just as Elizabeth had expected it. In others, it had been quite different.

The house was surrounded by a holly hedge, and it looked like the kind of place where any family might live. Elizabeth could easily imagine big Thanksgiving dinners being served in its large dining room, and a glistening Christmas tree set by the bay window in the front parlor. In the backyard were swing sets and a sandbox. Inside, children's drawings were tacked up everywhere and the furniture, although old, was comfortable. But in spite of its cozy appearance, Elizabeth and Enid had sensed the despair that drove people to seek out the Sanctuary.

The telephone rang, bringing Elizabeth back to the present. She didn't get up to answer it, knowing that Jessica had probably already pounced on the other extension. Sure enough, there was just one ring, then a pause, then a shout from outside Elizabeth's door.

"Liz! It's for you!"

A few moments later, Elizabeth spoke into the receiver. "Hello?"

"Hi, Liz," Enid said. "Making any progress on your article?"

Elizabeth sighed. "I haven't started," she admitted. "As a matter of fact, I can't seem to write about the shelter at all, even in my journal."

"Maybe you need to do something fun today and put yesterday's experience out of your mind for a while. It might give you a little perspective."

"You may be right," Elizabeth replied. "What did you have in mind?"

"A movie, the mall, the beach—you name it," Enid said.

"How about tennis at the park?" Elizabeth said. "I think some physical activity might clear my head and make me feel better."

"Sure," Enid responded readily. "Meet you there in twenty minutes."

Elizabeth hung up the telephone, put her journal and pen away, and took her tennis racquet from the closet. She knew her mother, Todd, and Enid were right. It was important for her to keep things in perspective.

Mr. Krezenski raised his bushy white eyebrows and gazed at Sara and Amanda with obvious displeasure. The dance instructor, who had fled Eastern Europe long before the Berlin Wall had come down, was a strict, no-nonsense sort of man. Not too long before, Jessica Wakefield had studied with him in preparation for her performance in the Miss Teen Sweet Valley pageant. Sara and Amanda, both dedicated to modern dance, took private lessons together on Sunday afternoons in addition to attending Mr. Krezenski's regular classes.

"You are not concentrating," Mr. Krezenski scolded.

Sara and Amanda glanced at each other uncomfortably.

"We'll try harder," Amanda promised in a quiet voice.

Mr. Krezenski started his ancient record player again, but Sara could not keep her mind on the dance. She was too concerned about Tim's pending arrival in Sweet Valley. It was just a matter of time before everyone at school would know she had lied about her brother having chosen to stay with their father after the divorce, and about his being popular and smart and a terrific athlete. Now the other kids were going to find out the truth: Tim Eastborne was a misfit and a dropout and a criminal.

Sara bit her lower lip and tried hard to concentrate on the steps Mr. Krezenski had choreographed. Somehow, she managed to get through the rest of the lesson without any more mistakes.

In the dressing room the girls changed from their leotards and tights into jeans and T-shirts. Standing in front of the ripply old mirror, they took their hair down from the customary chignons. Sara combed her dark tresses with her fingers, while Amanda used a brush for her thick auburn hair, each careful not to look at the other while they finished dressing.

When Sara finally reached for her dance bag, hurting so much inside that she didn't trust herself to speak, Amanda stopped her.

"Wait," she said. "Sara, let's talk."

Sara didn't dare say a word. She wanted to tell Amanda everything, but she was just too afraid.

"I wish you'd tell me what's bothering you," Amanda said calmly. She took her friend's arm and gently pressed her into one of the rickety wooden folding chairs that stood against the dressing-room wall. Then she sat down beside her. "It can't be that bad."

Sara's hazel eyes brimmed with tears and she shook her head.

Amanda rested her hand on Sara's shoulder. "It's OK, Sara. If you don't want to talk about it, we won't. But I just want you to know that I really value your friendship and I'm sorry about the way things have been going lately. I'd like to just go on like we were before."

Relief washed over Sara. She nodded, made a sound that was both a laugh and a sob, and hugged Amanda briefly.

Afterward the two girls went to the mall for a pizza. "It's incredible how much Elizabeth and Jessica look alike, isn't it?" Amanda said after they had ordered. On the way in, they had caught a glimpse of Jessica, dressed up in a formal, a sash, and a tiara, in front of a new fast-food place on the lower level of the mall. She had been passing out fliers to passers-by, and her smile had seemed a little forced.

Sara shrugged. "Well, they *are* identical twins," she said. The word *twins* brought her mind right back to the subject that was troubling her the most. Her own twin was about to spoil the life she had built so carefully.

"Still," Amanda persisted, lifting a piece of

pepperoni from her slice of pizza and popping it into her mouth, "it's quite a phenomenon, when you think about it. I mean, two people conceived together and born together. Two separate individuals so much alike that if they didn't wear different kinds of clothes and style their hair differently, a person couldn't tell them apart."

Sara ran the tip of her tongue nervously over her lips. "Twins do have a special bond," she said. She did not want to pursue the subject, but the words seemed to just tumble out of her mouth before she could stop them. "Sometimes it's almost spooky."

Amanda picked up her fork, stabbed one of the cherry tomatoes in her salad, and chewed it. "What do you mean, 'spooky'?" she asked.

"Well, when we were little, Tim and I used to have our own language. It wasn't just gibberish, either. Every word had a meaning." Sara laughed as she remembered. "It drove my mom and dad crazy! They were always telling us to speak plain English. We tried to cooperate, but when we were alone we always ended up using our own language."

"That's fascinating." Amanda leaned forward and put her elbows on the table. "Were the words consistent, or did you make up new ones as you went along?"

"They were always the same," Sara replied. "It was as though Tim and I were both born knowing them."

"Life is full of mysteries." Amanda smiled. "I'd like to meet Tim. When is he coming out to California to visit you and your mom?"

Sara swallowed hard, her momentary happiness scattering like a flock of birds. "He'll be here on Friday afternoon," she said after a long and difficult moment. "He's decided to live with us for a while."

Amanda's eyes lit up. "That's great!" she cried. "Why didn't you tell me sooner?"

"I just found out," Sara said. *That much, at least, is true,* she thought. She had only learned the night before that Tim was coming to live in Sweet Valley, and she was still reeling from the shock.

"You don't seem very happy about it," Amanda noted. She leaned forward even farther and narrowed her eyes. "Don't you and Tim get along anymore?"

Once again, Sara longed to tell Amanda everything, but in the end her courage failed her. Every time she was about to open up to Amanda, she remembered Darlene. Darlene had been her best friend back in Connecticut. When Tim had been arrested for stealing a car, Darlene had suddenly stopped speaking to Sara. She had moved her things out of the locker they shared, and told everyone in school that the Eastbornes were "the wrong kind of people." And because Darlene was popular, many of the other kids had taken their lead from her and snubbed Sara, too.

Sara finished her soda. "We get along all right," she lied.

Just then, Jerry "Crunch" McAllister, a former Sweet Valley High student, stopped by the table, wearing jeans, a football jersey, and a letterman's jacket. Jerry worked for a local construction company. He was good-looking in a macho sort of way. He was also crazy about Amanda.

"Hi, Amanda," he said. He pulled a chair over from another table and sat down without being invited. Sara knew Amanda wasn't interested in him; they had absolutely nothing in common. Amanda liked books and dancing and movies and school, and Jerry rarely talked about anything other than his van, which was gleaming purple with a roaring lion boldly painted on the side.

"Hello, Jerry," Amanda said.

Jerry nodded a halfhearted hello to Sara and turned to Amanda. "If you need a ride home," he said hopefully, "my wheels are right outside."

Jerry's "wheels" are always right outside, Sara reflected wryly. It was a wonder he didn't post armed guards around the van whenever he had to leave it unattended.

Amanda smiled. "My mother is picking us up," she said. "But thanks anyway." She glanced at her watch, raised her eyebrows, and looked meaningfully at Sara. "In fact, she's probably waiting for us right now. We'd better go."

"Right," Sara said quickly, hiding a smile as she grabbed her dance bag and stood up. "Nice seeing you again, Jerry."

Sara was sure that Jerry hadn't heard a word she had said. He was staring at Amanda, looking baffled, disappointed, and bewitched, all at the same time.

"That guy would walk barefoot over burning coals for you," Sara teased as the two girls rode the mall escalator to the first floor.

Amanda rolled her eyes. "He's such a jock," she whispered.

"Some girls like them," Sara replied. For a moment she thought of Bob. He was into athletics in a big way, and she was wild about him. Usually.

"I guess it all depends on the jock in question," Amanda answered with a shrug.

Elizabeth met Mrs. Marstowe after school on Monday in the coffee room at the community center. She wanted to expand her article on battered women to a series on troubled families that would deal with how families were affected by alcoholism and other addictions. She had asked Mrs. Marstowe if she could sit in on a few self-help meetings, and Mrs. Marstowe had readily agreed.

"You're sure I won't be interfering?" Elizabeth asked.

Mrs. Marstowe smiled. "I'm sure, Elizabeth." Her eyes dropped to the notebook and pencil in Elizabeth's hand. "You might want to leave those things with me, though. The kids will be uncomfortable if they think you're taking notes on what they say."

Without hesitation, Elizabeth handed the notebook and pencil to Mrs. Marstowe. "I'll just listen," she promised.

The social worker nodded and led the way out into the hall. Project Youth, where Amy and Barry worked as telephone counselors, was at one end of the building, and the general meeting room was at the other.

"We have several meetings a week here," Mrs. Marstowe explained quietly as they walked toward a pair of double doors. "Alcoholics Anonymous, Overeaters Anonymous, Al-Anon. There are even groups for people with gambling problems and for smokers. These days, there's a twelve-step group for practically every problem."

"Weren't the Twelve Steps originated by Alcoholics Anonymous?" Elizabeth asked.

Mrs. Marstowe paused outside the doors to the meeting room and smiled again. "Yes and no. A.A. was the first group to use the Steps as we know them today, but they're based on sound psychological and spiritual principles. They've been around, in one form or another, for a long, long time."

Elizabeth could hear people laughing and talking inside the room. "What about this particular group?"

"These kids use the Twelve Steps as guidelines, but it's sort of an informal gathering. You'll see what I mean." With that, Mrs. Marstowe gestured toward the doors, gave Elizabeth a reassuring smile, then turned and walked away.

After a moment's hesitation, Elizabeth drew a deep breath and walked into the meeting room.

Folding chairs had been set up in a big circle, and most of them were already filled. Elizabeth scanned the room and recognized Tom McKay. Tom was a junior at Sweet Valley High. Recently he had told Elizabeth that he thought he might be gay.

Tom smiled shyly at Elizabeth and moved his windbreaker so that she could sit down in the chair beside his.

"Hi," he said quietly as Elizabeth joined him.

A few minutes later the meeting began. Elizabeth settled back in her chair to listen thoughtfully as the group shared their problems, their experiences, and their hopes.

On Friday afternoon, when Sara arrived home from school, her brother was sitting in the living room with her mother. The two of them were laughing and talking.

Sara paused in the doorway, holding her books tightly against her chest. Tim was leaner and taller than she remembered, and his shoulders were broader. He was handsome, she realized, with his shiny brown hair and green eyes.

Still, Sara didn't want to get to know the "new" Tim; she didn't want to have to deal with him at all. But here he was, in the flesh, and because Bob was standing right behind her she couldn't even let her true feelings show.

When Tim saw his sister staring at him, he smiled shyly and stood. "Hello, Sari," he said, using his childhood nickname for her. His voice was a little hoarse.

"Hi." Sara set her books down on a small table just inside the door. She was shaking so badly, she folded her arms across her chest to steady herself. "I thought you weren't coming until tonight," she said coldly. *If I'd known you'd be here now, I wouldn't have brought Bob home,* she added to herself.

Tim shrugged. "There was a seat open on an earlier plane, so I grabbed it."

Bob stepped around Sara and looked at Tim in a way that made her a little nervous. Bob was clearly sizing her brother up, assigning him a value in his mind.

"I'm Bob Hillman," her boyfriend said, holding out a hand in greeting.

Tim returned the handshake confidently. "Tim Eastborne," he answered. His green eyes strayed from Bob to Sara. He started to say something, then stopped himself.

"I'm sure you've got some unpacking or something to do," Sara said quickly. She was uncomfortable with Bob and Tim being in the same room together. There were too many things that could go wrong. "Don't let us keep you."

For a second Tim looked surprised. Then he looked hurt. "Right. I have a lot to do. But Sara?"

Already on her way to the kitchen, Bob close beside her, Sara paused but did not turn around. She hoped the painful tension she felt didn't show in the set of her shoulders. "Yes?"

"I'd appreciate it if you could give me a little time tonight, or maybe tomorrow. I'd like to talk to you about some things."

It was then that Mrs. Eastborne spoke for the first time since Sara's arrival. "Of course Sara can spare a few hours," she called out from the living room. Her tone was pointed but kind. "After all, you're her brother."

Sara continued on to the kitchen. She opened the refrigerator and took out two cans of soda for herself and Bob.

Bob was frowning at her when she handed him a soda. "All week long the kids at school have been talking about your brother coming to Sweet Valley, but you haven't said anything about him. Why is that, Sara?"

Sara took a sip of her soda and fixed her attention on the dripping faucet in the sink. It seemed she couldn't look anyone straight in the eye anymore. For the thousandth time, she asked herself what would happen if she told Bob the whole truth, and for the thousandth time she came up with the same answer. Bob would be like Darlene and the other kids back in Connecticut. Once he found out what kind of person Tim was, he wouldn't want anything to do with any of the Eastbornes.

"We don't get along very well," she finally answered.

"He seems nice enough," Bob replied. "At least he has good taste. Those running shoes he's wearing are the best on the market."

Sara sighed. *Guys like Tim need good running shoes,* she thought, *for making quick getaways.*

Bob left soon after finishing his soda. When he had gone, Tim wandered into the kitchen and opened the refrigerator door.

"Dad says hello," he said as he took out a package of cheddar cheese, a stick of margarine, and a loaf of bread.

As she watched Tim, Sara remembered with a certain unwelcome tenderness how her twin had loved to make them grilled cheese sandwiches when they were kids. "You actually saw him?" she asked, aware that her tone was a little tart.

Tim smiled. "He's the same as ever—all business. But it took a parent to sign me out of Rivercrest, and Mom was too far away to be stuck with the job."

Although she felt a sudden pang of sympathy for her brother, Sara wouldn't allow herself to soften. Her attitude was the only real protection she had against Tim and the special talent he had for hurting and embarrassing her. "I guess if you hadn't gotten into trouble in the first place, it wouldn't have been a problem," she said.

Her brother sighed. "Sara . . ."

Sara glared at him. "I'm surprised they let you leave. Aren't you supposed to stay in the state when you're on probation?"

Tim looked Sara directly in the eye. "I'll be seeing a probation officer here," he said quietly.

And everyone in Sweet Valley will know, Sara though bitterly.

"Great," she muttered as she stormed out of the kitchen. "That's just great!"

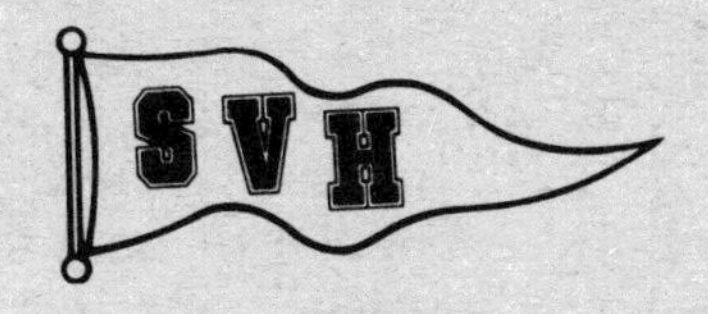

Four

As Mrs. Eastborne brought her car to a stop at the beach, Sara looked out over the shore. The sunlight seemed to shatter into dazzling, dancing fragments as it struck the water.

"I'm sorry about getting you up so early on a Saturday morning," Mrs. Eastborne said. "But I think you and I need to have a heart-to-heart talk."

Sara sighed, unsnapped her seat belt, and got out of the car. The cool ocean breeze danced in her long brown hair as she stood gazing at the Pacific, her hands stuffed into the pockets of her lightweight jacket. She knew her mother wanted to talk about Tim, and she dreaded the whole discussion.

"OK," she said reluctantly.

Mother and daughter walked down a set of

wooden steps that led to the beach. Gulls swooped and dove against the bright blue sky. The frothy tide rolled toward the shore as Sara and Mrs. Eastborne strolled along its edge.

"I know Tim has caused you a lot of problems in the past," Mrs. Eastborne began.

"That's an understatement," Sara murmured. Her words were sarcastic, but her tone was polite. She knew it wasn't her mother's fault that Tim had gone bad. *She* had done her best.

Mrs. Eastborne sighed and tucked her hands into the back pockets of her jeans. "Sara, it's time to let go of those old resentments and get on with your life. Tim is your brother, he's part of our family, and he needs us more now than he ever has."

Sara felt her cheeks burn with anger. She should have known her mother would be fooled by Tim's stylish haircut, his new way of dressing, his gentler, more vulnerable manner. Well, she wasn't going to let her twin con *her* the way he had their mother.

"Why did he have to come here?" she burst out miserably. "Why couldn't Tim have stayed in Connecticut with Dad? Now he's going to be seeing a probation officer and everybody is going to know what he's done—"

"Sara," Mrs. Eastborne interrupted gently, linking her arm with her daughter's. "Suppose you'd been the one to get into trouble?

Wouldn't you want to be able to depend on Tim and me to stand by you?"

Sara shook her head. "The point is, I *didn't* break the law and get myself arrested and thrown into reform school."

"No, Sara," Mrs. Eastborne argued patiently, "that isn't the point. Tim belongs to us, and as long as he's honestly trying to straighten out his life, we owe him our support."

A tear streaked Sara's cheek, and she wiped it away with the back of her hand. *Why* couldn't Tim have stayed in Connecticut? "He doesn't need us," she sniffled furiously. "He needs Dad."

Mrs. Eastborne encircled Sara's shoulders with her arm. "You're a big girl now, Sara, and you know in your heart that your father can't be there for Tim. He's not a bad person, but he's very closed emotionally and I don't think he's going to change."

Sara couldn't help but think of Amanda's mother and father, who were deeply in love. The Hayes family was solid and secure and, not for the first time, Sara wished that she could change places with her friend. "What are you going to do when Tim steals another car, Mom?" she asked. "What if it's something worse?"

"Tim has changed," Mrs. Eastborne insisted. "If you'd just give him a chance, you'd see that he's not the same person he was before. He's been working very hard to get well, Sara."

Sara pulled away from her mother and walked a little ahead. *If I give him another chance, he'll only disappoint me again,* Sara thought bitterly.

"I'll let you use the car for a whole week," Jessica bargained from her seat on the long counter in the bathroom the twins shared. "And you can play my new Jamie Peters tape whenever you want."

"No," Elizabeth said firmly, dropping a pot of lip gloss into the makeup drawer. "I wouldn't pose as Miss Teen Sweet Valley if you offered me a Porsche, Jess. And who needs to borrow that tape when I can hear it blaring from your room every night?"

Jessica made a pouty face. "Liz, this is *important.* This is the biggest sale in the history of Sweet Valley, and I've still got half my allowance left because I never have time to *spend* it!" She paused and drew in her breath in preparation for another burst of persuasion. "Besides, think of the interesting things you might overhear at the Women's Club luncheon. You might come out of this with a whole *series* of articles for *The Oracle!"*

"I've already got a whole series planned," Elizabeth told her sister. "You're on your own, Jess. You're Miss Teen Sweet Valley, and you're going to have to live up to the title all by yourself. Sorry."

"You're not sorry!" Jessica accused as she followed Elizabeth into her room. A look of inspiration suddenly glowed in Jessica's face. "I'm sick!" she whimpered as she sank to the edge of Elizabeth's bed in a pretended fit of dizziness.

"Give it a rest," Elizabeth said. She gathered up her backpack and peered inside to make sure she had her set of car keys. She and Enid were planning to help out at the shelter, keeping a group of kids entertained while their mothers listened to a lecture on preparing résumés. At the door, she looked back at her dejected sister. "If you want to skip the Women's Club luncheon, call your runner-up and ask her to fill in for you. She won't appreciate having to make a speech on such short notice, but—"

"Never!" Jessica said, shooting off the bed like a rocket. "If I do that, someone might get the idea that I can't handle the job!"

Elizabeth raised an eyebrow and left.

Sara stared at the kitchen telephone, her chin propped in her hand. The house was empty. Her mother and Tim had gone to the mall to shop. She had to talk to someone about how she was feeling, she just *had* to, but who could she call?

Remembering an article Elizabeth Wakefield had written for *The Oracle* about the teen hotline at Project Youth, Sara reached for the receiver, called information, and got the number.

"Project Youth," a feminine voice answered warmly.

Sara bit her lower lip. The person sounded familiar. Was it someone she knew from school? Someone who would recognize her from what she said and spread the word about Tim all over Sweet Valley High?

"Hello?" the girl prompted. "Is someone there?"

Sara closed her eyes tightly. She needed so much to talk, but she was afraid. She replaced the receiver with a crash.

Twenty minutes later, Sara called again. This time a guy answered.

"Project Youth. What can I do for you?"

Sara's throat felt like it was in a knot, and her voice came out hoarse and scratchy. "I . . . I'd just like to talk for a few minutes. If that's all right."

"That's what we're here for. What's your name?"

"Sara." There were lots of Saras at Sweet Valley High. If she didn't identify herself further, she reasoned, this person wouldn't be able to guess which one she was.

"I'm Barry," he responded. "So tell me, what's going on with you?"

The words just spilled out of Sara. She told Barry about her brother, changing Tim's name to Mark just in case, and about her parents' divorce. She talked about losing her friends over "Mark's" actions when they lived back East, and about how afraid she was that history would repeat itself. When she had finished pouring out the entire story, she waited.

"Is that everything?" Barry asked kindly.

"Yes," Sara said shakily. "What's your advice?"

Barry chuckled. "We don't give advice, Sara. Usually the people who call us only need to talk out something with someone who will listen. Often they have the answers right inside them. It's just that they don't want to look at them squarely, that's all."

Sara thanked Barry for listening and hung up.

There were eight kids gathered in the big backyard at the Sanctuary, watching Elizabeth and Enid with round, troubled eyes.

Elizabeth swallowed the lump that rose in her throat, smiled, and clapped her hands together. "OK, gang, we're going to have relay races."

Enid was the leader of the red team, and Elizabeth the leader of the blue. For over an hour the girls conducted a spirited backyard Olympics, and at the end of the games it was decided that the blue and red teams had performed equally well. Elizabeth gave each of the kids a brightly colored balloon as a prize, and when the lecture for the mothers was over, she genuinely regretted having to leave.

After dropping Enid off at home, Elizabeth met Todd for an afternoon movie. He kissed her lightly on the cheek when she joined him in the lobby of the theater, then handed her a bag of popcorn. "Hi, Liz," he said, in a voice that made her feel soft inside. "Know what? I see the problems of the whole world in your eyes."

Elizabeth laughed and let her forehead rest against his strong shoulder for a moment. "I've already had this lecture from my mom," she said.

Todd took her free hand and started toward the theater's inner doors. "What lecture is that?" he teased.

"You know," Elizabeth confessed. "The one about not letting myself get too caught up in other people's problems."

His eyes danced. "Oh, *that* lecture," he said as he and Elizabeth sat down in the still-bright theater. "It must be pretty tough, seeing all that suffering."

"You've got that right," she agreed, reaching into her popcorn bag. "I just spent an hour with eight little kids who've probably seen more action than your average soldier."

"Did they have a good time?" Todd asked. "The kids, I mean."

"Sure they did," Elizabeth answered. "Enid and I organized our own Olympics, and everybody was a winner." She remembered how the children had played on the Sanctuary's green lawn, their laughter like a song in the warm air, and she felt better.

The lights went down, and an advertisement for the snack bar filled the screen. Elizabeth slipped her hand into Todd's and gave his fingers a tight squeeze.

On Saturday night Bob called Sara just before he was supposed to pick her up. He said he had to cancel their date for that evening because his father had invited an important client to dinner and Bob felt he should join his family.

Sara couldn't help but wonder if Bob had already heard something about Tim's past. Sara tried to control the pain in her voice as she told him she didn't mind.

Sara had been avoiding Tim since his arrival, but now that Bob had canceled their date, she was going to have to have dinner with him. She knew from the look in her mother's eyes that there would be no getting out of it.

"Mom told me about the awards you've won for your dancing," Tim ventured when the Eastbornes were seated around the dining room table. "That's terrific, Sara. I'll bet you're really proud."

Sara shrugged and concentrated on buttering her dinner roll. "I guess."

"Tim was telling me he took some art classes

while he was at Rivercrest," Mrs. Eastborne said, a bit too eagerly. "He thinks he might like to go into advertising someday."

Tim laughed. "Mom," he said good-naturedly, "please don't talk about me like I'm not here. I can speak for myself."

Sara ignored the exchange between her mother and brother and took a drink of water.

"Tell me about your friend Amanda," Tim said. "Mom says you two take dance classes together."

"She's nice," Sara said grudgingly. She didn't want to talk about her friend with Tim. She didn't even want to be in the same room with him.

Mrs. Eastborne excused herself to bring in dessert. When she had left the room, Sara laid down her fork and pushed away her plate.

"It's nice of you to be so concerned about my friends and my life, Tim," she said with acid sweetness. "Too bad you won't let me keep them. You'll probably drive them off the way you did Darlene and the others."

Tim flinched. "Sara, will you just give me a chance? I know I've hurt you in the past, but I'm different now, and—"

"Listen," Sara broke in, her voice a fierce whisper, "I don't want you to tell anybody about Rivercrest, understand? I told everyone at school that you were living with Dad in Connecticut, that you get good grades, and that you're a member of the track team. And you'd better go along with that story."

Tim's eyes flashed. "You want me to lie?"

"It wouldn't be the first time, would it?" she countered.

Tim placed his hands on the table as if to steady himself. He looked carefully at his sister, and then spoke. "Sara, if I learned anything by going to Alcoholics Anonymous meetings, it's that lies and secrets make a person sick. I *need* to be straight with people about where I've been and what I've done."

"Terrific," Sara hissed. "Go to A.A. and be as honest as you want! But I'll never forgive you if you don't back up my story at Sweet Valley High!"

"I have a feeling you'll never forgive me anyway," Tim replied sadly. He pushed back his chair just as Mrs. Eastborne came in with a cherry pie, his favorite dessert. "OK, Sara." Tim stood up and looked down at his sister's flushed face. "I want to make up to you for the things I did. So I'll do what you want, even though I think it's crazy." Tim nodded to his mother and left the room.

Mrs. Eastborne set the pie in the middle of the table. "What happened?" she asked quietly.

Sara left her chair and began to clear the table. "We reached an understanding," she replied, avoiding her mother's eyes.

Elizabeth brought the car to a stop outside the community center, switched on the interior light, and consulted the schedule Mrs. Marstowe had given her. According to the schedule, there was an open A.A. meeting, which meant that non-members were welcome, starting at seven-thirty. After the meeting, she would drive to Todd's house.

Elizabeth found the meeting room easily. The place was filled with smoke, the scent of strong coffee, laughter, and talk. She glanced around the room and saw that what Mrs. Marstowe had told her was true. All kinds of people—young and old, rich and poor, men and women—went to A.A. meetings.

Elizabeth quietly took a seat, and before long the program began. This time, instead of being set in a circle, the chairs had been set out in rows in front of a podium. A woman in jeans and a T-shirt got up and stood before the group.

"Hi," she said clearly. "My name's Jeanine, and I'm an alcoholic."

"Hi, Jeanine!" the audience thundered back, their greeting filled with warmth and acceptance.

Jeanine opened a book and began to read from it. After the opening, the actual meeting began. The topic of the night was honesty, and Elizabeth quickly became fascinated by the friendliness of the people.

A young guy a few rows ahead stood up. "My name is Tim," he said, "and I'm an alcoholic."

Elizabeth had already figured out that saying "I'm an alcoholic" after introducing oneself was a way of admitting one had a problem with drinking.

A loud "Hi, Tim!" rocked the room.

Elizabeth listened closely as Tim started to talk about how he had just moved to California from another state, where he had been in a lot of trouble. He was living with his mother and sister now, and his mother was really knocking herself out to make him feel welcome. His sister, on the other hand, could hardly stand to be in the same room with him, and she wanted him to lie about his past because she was ashamed of him. When he was through with his story he said, "And that's where I am right now," and then sat down.

Tim's story touched Elizabeth, and stayed in her mind while several other people took turns talking to the group. She and Jessica and Steven had had problems getting along at various times in their lives, but never had they felt ashamed of one another. Elizabeth couldn't imagine the pain Tim must have been feeling.

Midway through the meeting there was a break. Elizabeth's first impulse was to leave, but she forced herself to stay. If she wanted credibility as a journalist someday, she told herself, she had to maintain the habit of seeing things through.

Tim came up to her as she was standing by the refreshment table munching on a cookie.

"Hi," he said. He wriggled his eyebrows comically. "Come here often?"

Elizabeth laughed. "I'm a visitor," she said,

putting out her free hand. "My name is Elizabeth—"

"Uh-huh, Elizabeth," he interrupted. "We don't use last names here."

Elizabeth's cheeks burned slightly. "Sorry. I forgot. But I know I'm not supposed to talk about what people say in this room."

Tim grinned. "I'll probably see you around school. I'll be joining the junior class at Sweet Valley High on Monday." He paused. "Or are you in college?"

Elizabeth shook her head. "No, I'm a junior at Sweet Valley High, too."

The meeting started again and Elizabeth returned to her chair. Though she tried to pay attention to the speakers, her eyes kept glancing over to the back of Tim's head. *What is it about him that reminds me of someone else?* she wondered.

When the meeting was over, Tim walked her to her car.

"I suppose it's too much to hope that you don't have a boyfriend," he teased. Tim's manner was friendly and funny, not threatening in any way.

Elizabeth smiled. "I'm going with somebody," she answered. "But we can be friends. A person can't have too many of those!"

Tim made a pouty face. "So you won't dump this guy, huh?"

Elizabeth laughed. "Not a chance." Tim opened the Fiat's door for her and she slid behind the wheel. "Look me up on Monday, though, and I'll introduce you around."

"Thanks," Tim said hoarsely.

As she drove away from the curb, Elizabeth tooted the horn. *He showed an awful lot of emotion in that one little word,* she thought sadly.

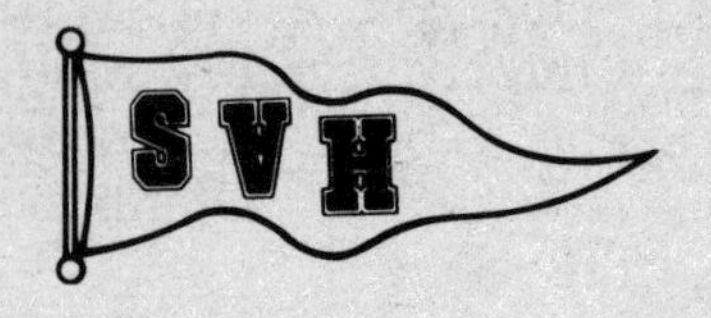

Five

On Monday morning, Tim turned up in one of Elizabeth's early classes.

Elizabeth had expected to see Tim around school, but she was caught off balance all the same. After all, only two days before, she had heard Tim pour out his heart in an A.A. meeting. Suddenly, she had the strange feeling that just by being in the class with him now, she had somehow betrayed him.

"Hi," Tim said as he sat down at the desk behind hers.

"Hello, Tim." She turned to Todd, who was sitting across the aisle from her. "This is Todd Wilkins."

Tim grinned. "So you must be the guy Elizabeth told me about. You're a lucky man," he said to Todd.

Todd grinned back at Tim and offered his

hand. "Welcome to Sweet Valley High," he said. "You're obviously a man of taste and refinement."

The bell rang before Tim could say anything in response, and the chatter-filled room lapsed into a gradual silence. The teacher consulted his notes and then focused his attention on the new student in the room.

"Tim Eastborne?"

Elizabeth's new friend lifted his hand to acknowledge the question.

The instructor looked at some papers on his desk. "I see you're a transfer student from Hillview, Connecticut. Welcome to California."

"Thank you," Tim said politely.

Elizabeth glanced around the room and noticed that most of the girls were studying Tim appreciatively. All except Sara Eastborne, that is. She was staring out the window, and there was a pink tinge to her cheeks.

Eastborne. Of course. Tim must be Sara's brother, Elizabeth realized. *But why is Sara acting so strange?* When Tim had come into the classroom earlier, Elizabeth had seen him try to catch Sara's eye. Sara had ignored him.

The teacher began the day's lesson. Elizabeth tried to concentrate on the class, but she was working out another equation in her mind. At the meeting Saturday night, Tim had admitted he had a drinking problem. And he had said his sister was ashamed of him and wanted him to keep his past a secret.

A deep sadness touched Elizabeth's heart.

Tim was a nice guy, and it seemed to her that he was trying hard to straighten out his life. He needed support from his family, not anger.

When the bell rang, Todd left immediately for his next class. Sara rushed out of the room without so much as looking at Tim, her jaw clamped down tightly. Elizabeth had a rare free period next and she had planned to spend it in the *Oracle* office, mapping out the first article of her series. But she decided to stay and talk to Tim for a few minutes.

"You're Sara's brother," Elizabeth said quietly.

When Tim turned his eyes to her, he looked miserable. "Yeah. But the stuff I said the other night . . ."

"I know." Elizabeth was quick to reassure him. "It's a secret. You don't need to worry that I'll say anything."

"Thanks." Tim gathered his books and stood up. He hesitated, then cleared his throat. "Maybe we could talk sometime."

Elizabeth smiled. "Sure."

When they reached the hallway, Elizabeth introduced Tim to some of the other students. Everyone seemed to like him immediately, especially the girls.

"Who's the hunk?" Jessica asked, leaning close to Elizabeth to whisper the words out of the side of her mouth.

"Tim Eastborne," Elizabeth answered. Tim turned at the sound of his name. His face lit up with mischievous pleasure when he saw Jessica.

"Do my eyes deceive me?" he said. "Are there really *two* of you?"

Elizabeth saw that Jessica was charmed by Tim's good looks and outgoing personality. Her sister beamed at him. "We're identical twins," she said.

Elizabeth shook her head. "He never would have guessed that, Jess," she teased. "Tim, meet the one and only Jessica Wakefield."

Another bell rang before Jessica could carry the introduction any further, and the crowd in the hall thinned out rapidly.

Elizabeth went on to the *Oracle* office, where she found Penny Ayala going over the latest issue of the paper. Penny was tall and lanky, with warm brown hair and hazel eyes.

"Hi, Liz," she greeted her friend and colleague. "What's the scoop?"

"There's a new guy in school," she answered. "We could do the usual profile."

Penny gathered some files from her desk and looked carefully at Elizabeth. "Is this Tim Eastborne, Sara's brother?"

Elizabeth nodded. "He's nice."

Penny glanced toward the door to make sure it was closed. "He's been in trouble, Liz. One of my sources told me he was in reform school before he came to Sweet Valley. He stole a car once, it seems, and he had some scrapes with the law over alcohol and drugs."

"This source of yours," Elizabeth asked, "will she—or he—keep this information confidential, or is it going to be spread all over school?"

Penny drummed her fingers on the surface of her desk. "Knowing this person, I'd say the word has a good chance of getting out," she said regretfully. "Gossip like that is just too juicy for some people to keep to themselves."

Sara would never have introduced Tim and Amanda if she had been given a choice in the matter. But Amanda had dragged her aside in the hallway after the last bell of the day, pointed in Tim's direction, and whispered, "Is that your brother?"

"Yes," Sara admitted glumly.

Amanda's tawny eyes danced. "I want to meet him."

"Look, the two of you wouldn't have anything in common."

"*Sara,*" Amanda complained.

Sara sighed. "OK. Come on."

Amanda followed her friend across the wide hallway to Tim's locker, where he was struggling with his combination lock.

"Tim?"

At the sound of his sister's voice, Tim turned in surprise. The look of happiness on his face made Sara feel guilty about the way she had been treating him.

But only for a moment.

Sara drew a deep breath. "Tim, this is Amanda Hayes, my best friend," she said, putting just the slightest emphasis on the last three words. "Amanda, my brother, Tim."

Amanda smiled and tossed her pretty auburn hair back over one shoulder. Her beautiful eyes sparkled as she looked at Tim.

While Tim and Amanda were chatting with each other, Sara thought fast. Her mother had loaned her the car that morning so Sara could show Tim around Sweet Valley after school. Now all Sara wanted to do was get rid of her brother before he slipped and said something she didn't want Amanda to know about.

"I'm sorry, Tim," she blurted out, interrupting his conversation with Amanda. "But I have to meet with my English teacher about an assignment I missed, so I won't be able to give you that tour of town after all."

"I'd be happy to show you around town," Amanda said warmly. "I have my mom's car today."

The invisible energy crackling back and forth between Amanda and Tim made Sara cry out, "No!" She was terrified of what her best friend and her brother might talk about while they were alone.

"What?" Amanda asked.

Tim said nothing, but his eyes showed his hurt. He understood Sara's objection only too well.

"Well, i-it's just that . . . I thought you had a dance lesson to make up after school today," Sara said.

Amanda frowned. "No, I don't," she said, obviously confused.

"Listen, it's OK," Tim said quickly. "I'll just

go home and mow the lawn or something." He smiled shyly at his sister's best friend. "It was nice meeting you, Amanda."

"Wait," Amanda said firmly as Tim turned to walk away.

Tim paused and looked back at Amanda.

"I *don't* have a dance lesson today," Amanda told him. She turned to look at Sara for a moment and then turned back to Tim. "Still want to experience Sweet Valley, California, on zero dollars a day?"

Tim laughed. "That's right in my price range," he answered. "Let's go."

Sara was seething, but there wasn't much she could do or say without looking like even more of a fool than she already did. She sent Tim a scorching glance and felt a certain satisfaction when she saw him flinch.

"See you later, Sara," Amanda said. She and Tim left the school together, leaving Sara staring after them in frustration and helpless fury.

Sara waited tensely for Tim to come home later that afternoon. When he did, he was whistling and, for the first time since his arrival in Sweet Valley, he seemed happy. When he came into the kitchen and found Sara there, tossing a salad she was making for dinner, he stopped short.

"I didn't say anything to Amanda about my

past," he said in a strained voice. "So you can stop worrying about it."

Again Sara felt a twinge of guilt, but she wouldn't let Tim see how she felt. She continued to toss the salad and said nothing.

Tim took a small bottle of orange juice from the refrigerator and broke the seal. "Sari," he said, "Amanda is a really nice girl. Don't you think it would be better if you told her the truth about everything? Then you wouldn't have to worry that the friendship was about to come crashing down around you."

Sara whirled around to face her brother.

"Better for whom, Tim? For you? I'm *not* telling Amanda anything about the car you stole, or about your drinking problem, or about the drugs you used to take, or about your time at Rivercrest. And you'd better not tell her, either!"

Tim leaned against the counter and rested his forehead in his palm. "You're making a mistake," he said finally, in a quiet but insistent voice. "The truth always comes out, Sari."

"It doesn't have to," Sara replied stubbornly.

Tim sighed raggedly, then straightened and took a greedy drink from his bottle of juice. "Remember how mad Dad used to get when we talked to each other in our private language?"

The unexpected change of subject caught Sara unaware. She tried not to smile, but she couldn't help it. Mr. Eastborne had found his children's method of communication annoying, to say the least. "I remember," she said softly, and—for just a second—it was as though the old, untroubled Tim was standing there in the kitchen with her.

"Hello!" Mrs. Eastborne called from the living room. "I'm home!"

The brief flicker of understanding between the Eastborne twins was gone.

"Don't think you're going to get out of taking your turn at fixing dinner just because you're a guy," Mrs. Eastborne teased as she came into the kitchen. Her happy look faded rapidly when she picked up on the tension that filled the room.

"I made a beef casserole," Sara said stiffly when the silence had grown too long for everyone's comfort.

"Smells good," Mrs. Eastborne said softly. She looked from her daughter to her son with a sad expression in her eyes. "What am I going to do with the two of you?"

Tim shrugged and left the kitchen. Sara turned back to the salad.

Mrs. Eastborne made herself a cup of tea in the microwave before speaking again.

"You've got to stop fighting the situation and accept the fact that Tim is back in our lives to stay," she said wearily as she sat down at the table. "I'm going to an Al-Anon meeting tonight. Would you like to go with me?"

Sara put on a quilted mitt and took the casserole from the oven. "I promised Bob I'd help him with his homework tonight," she said.

"What about your brother?" Mrs. Eastborne asked evenly. "When are you going to be willing to help *him*, Sara?"

Tears filled Sara's eyes. "All I want is to live my own life the way I want," she answered firmly.

When the Eastbornes sat down to dinner a few minutes later, Tim was especially talkative.

"Sara's friend Amanda took me out to the beach today and showed me the college campus and the downtown area," he told their mother. "Why didn't somebody tell me the prettiest girls in the Western Hemisphere live right here in Sweet Valley? The Wakefield twins, Amanda—wow!"

Mrs. Eastborne smiled, and Sara felt guilty for having made her mother sad earlier, and jealous because Tim had been the one to bring a smile to her face now.

Tim helped himself to another serving of beef casserole. "Elizabeth is going to interview me for a profile in the school paper," he announced.

"She's going to write about you for *The Oracle?*" Sara asked loudly.

Tim nodded. "I guess it's the customary way to introduce the new kid," he said. "Don't worry, Sari. I won't tell Liz about my time in the big house."

" 'Liz'?" Sara echoed.

"I'm her friend," Tim stated simply. "I *am* allowed to have friends, aren't I, Sara? Or should I have cleared that with you first?"

The telephone rang before Sara could think of a reply. She muttered an excuse and rushed to answer it. "Hello?" she said impatiently.

"Hi, Sara, it's Bob. Listen, we're not going to be able to get together and study tonight after all. My mother is having some people in and I have to be here."

"I see," she said. *How much disappointment can I take in one night?* she thought as she tightened her grip on the phone.

"I'll drive you to school in the morning," Bob volunteered. "OK?"

"OK," Sara confirmed. When she hung up the phone, the tears that had gathered in her eyes began to fall freely. Without a word to her mother or brother, she went up to her room for the rest of the evening.

Tim and Elizabeth had agreed to meet in the cafeteria before classes started on Tuesday morning so she could interview him for *The Oracle*. She was waiting there when Tim came in.

"Hi," she said with a bright smile.

Tim sat down across the table from her. "You know, you act like I'm just another average kid going to Sweet Valley High," he said. "Doesn't it bother you, knowing what you do about me?"

"What *do* I know about you?" she countered.

"You know I've been in trouble, that my sister wishes I'd never come out here to live. . . ." Tim glanced around. The cafeteria was empty except for the two of them and the people working in the kitchen. "I was in reform school before I came here, Liz," he said. "I stole a car."

Elizabeth wasn't put off. Like any reporter worth her number-two pencils, she had good instincts about people, and she knew Tim Eastborne was basically a good person. "I guess it would probably be better if I didn't put that in the profile," she said with another smile.

Tim rolled his eyes. "Yeah. Sara would have a fit," he said. "And I guess I don't want the whole town to know."

"Maybe if you just keep doing what you've been doing since you've been here, things will get better between the two of you."

"Maybe," Tim answered uncertainly. "Now, let's get on with that interview!"

"OK. Tell me about your home town," Elizabeth said as she opened her notebook. "You lived in . . ."

"Connecticut," Tim said promptly. "We lived in a big white house. Behind it was a hill, and every winter Sara and I and the other kids in the neighborhood would be out there sledding and having snowball fights. One winter, we built a fort out of snow. It was big enough to walk around in!"

Elizabeth smiled and wrote hurriedly. "How about school? What did you like best about that?"

Tim's smile faded. "I have a slight learning disability," he said. "Sometimes it takes me a little longer to grasp things than it does the average person."

"I think Sara mentioned once that you were a star on your school's track team."

Tim looked puzzled. "The track team?"

Elizabeth nodded.

"Oh," Tim said after a moment. "The track team. Well, I wasn't exactly a star. I just sort of . . . ran."

Sensing the subject wasn't going to pan out, Elizabeth tried another angle. "How do you like California so far?"

Tim's smile became as warm as the bright sunshine pouring in through the windows. "It's great. Lives up to its reputation for producing really terrific-looking girls."

Elizabeth laughed. "And what would you like to do after you graduate? Are you planning to go to college?"

Tim shook his head. "College is more Sara's style. She's really smart. I'm more interested in vocational school. I'd like to work with cars, or maybe computers."

Elizabeth jotted some notes in her notebook, careful not to let her confusion show. First Tim had said he had a learning disability, and now he confessed that he didn't have much interest in college. Elizabeth could have sworn she had once heard Sara telling some kids that Tim was a sure bet to be valedictorian of his class, and that he planned to go to Harvard, just like his father had.

"What do *you* want to be?" Tim asked, the suddenness of his question taking Elizabeth by surprise.

"That's easy," she answered. "A journalist. I really like writing."

"That's great," Tim replied. "You know, I think Sara is going to be a world-class dancer. But then, she could be anything she wants to be," he said proudly. "A doctor, a lawyer, a rocket scientist. Anything."

"You really care a lot about your sister, don't you?" Elizabeth asked gently.

"Yeah," Tim replied. "Yeah, I care a lot."

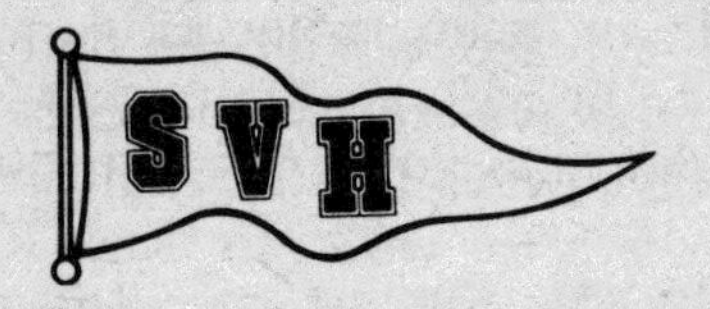

Six

By Friday, Sara could see that Tim was already popular with the students at Sweet Valley High. That worried her. She would have been much happier if her brother had kept to himself, but so far he had joined the photography club and had made a point of talking to everybody he met. Wherever he went, girls flirted with him, but he didn't seem to notice anyone but Amanda. *My best friend,* Sara thought bitterly.

Sara closed her locker door. As she turned to face the empty hallway, she felt an awful sense of loneliness. For the first time in months, her best friend wouldn't be going with her to dance class.

Sara lifted her chin. *It's ironic,* she thought. Tim was the one who had done everything wrong. He should be the real outcast. *I'm the good one, but I'm the one who's being left all alone! It's just not fair,* she thought. Tim and Amanda were together practically all the time, Amanda didn't seem to have any time for Sara anymore. And Bob was always finding fault with her.

Sara decided to walk to Mr. Krezenski's dance studio. She hadn't gone more than halfway when it began to rain.

It figures, Sara thought glumly as she hurried along the sidewalk, the rain soaking through her jeans and cotton shirt. It was one of those days when it seemed as if the whole universe was against her.

Mr. Krezenski greeted her with a sympathetic smile and a soft towel, and Sara hurried into the dressing room to dry off and change into her dance clothes.

"Where is Miss Hayes today?" the dance teacher inquired when she rejoined the class in the studio.

Sara sighed. "She's tutoring someone for a special test," she said. *My stupid brother,* she added mentally.

"I see." Mr. Krezenski went to his record player and put on one of the scratchy records he loved so much.

Sara began to move slowly with the music, letting it sweep her up in a mystical wave, letting it lift her out of herself. For the first time in days she felt a degree of peace, and her problems seemed to float away.

"Very good, Sara," Mr. Krezenski said when the music finally ebbed away and Sara came back from her mental travels. Mr. Krezenski was not extravagant with praise, and those words meant a lot to Sara. She felt a shaky smile settle on her mouth. "Thank you," she said quietly.

The old man nodded, excused the class with an affectionate gesture of his hand, then turned back to his beloved phonograph records. Sara went into the dressing room and changed back into her street clothes, which were still a little damp from the rain. She ignored the chatter of the other girls and hurried out.

Her heart was heavy as she peered through the rain-speckled glass of the studio's front window to see if her mother had remembered to pick her up. Sure enough, Mrs. Eastborne's convertible was parked at the curb, lights on, windshield wipers swishing back and forth. After stuffing her books into her dance bag with her tights, slippers, and leotard, Sara rushed through the storm and pulled open the car door.

Tim was sitting behind the wheel, and Sara's smile fell away as she settled into the passenger seat and fastened her seat belt.

" 'Hi, Tim,' " her brother teased in a squeaky, high-pitched voice. " 'Gee, it was nice of you to come and get me so I wouldn't have to walk home in the rain.' "

"Save it," Sara grumbled, pushing her damp

hair back from her face with both hands. "Since when are you allowed to drive? I thought they took your license away."

"I got it back for good behavior," Tim answered, unruffled. He looked into the side mirror as he pulled away from the curb. "It's my turn to cook, so I thought we'd pick up a pizza on the way home. It seems like the most merciful thing to do."

Sara fought back a grin. She had always had a weakness for Tim's sense of humor, but that didn't change the fact that she was angry at him for disrupting her life. "Pizza sounds good," she admitted grudgingly.

Tim brought the car to a stop at the light and kept his eyes straight ahead. "I'm sorry, Sari," he said. "If I could go back and change the things I did, I would."

"Talk is cheap," Sara said bitterly. How many times had Tim promised her that he would stop hanging around with such a bad crowd, stop getting into trouble, stop drinking? "Action is the only thing that counts with me."

The light changed and Tim eased through the intersection. The rain had become practically a deluge. "OK, fair enough. The problem is, I'm *trying* to show you that I've changed, but you won't pay any attention."

Sara let out a trembly sigh. "I believed in you once before, Tim. It cost me most of my friends."

Tim flipped the signal switch and turned into

the parking lot of the pizza place. "Coming in?" he asked, ignoring her last remark.

Sara was almost stubborn enough to wait in the car by herself, but the natural human desire for warmth and light and the company of other people won out. She opened the car door and dashed for the door to the pizza place.

Inside, Sara stood by a machine that was supposed to measure stress. After a moment's thought, she pulled a quarter from the pocket of her jeans and dropped it into the slot. She gripped the metal handle and a red light flashed to indicate that she had reached mind-blowing levels of anxiety. Sara smiled.

"Is the top of your head going to fly off?" Tim inquired, his eyes twinkling.

"I'll survive," she said, once again caught between the desire to laugh with him and to scorn him.

Tim cocked a thumb toward the video games. "Come on. I'll beat you at Golden Axe while we're waiting for our order."

"In your dreams," Sara answered before she could stop herself. *Just for now, I'll pretend that this Tim is the old Tim and that everything is normal,* she thought as she followed him toward the video games.

When Tim and Sara arrived home a short time later, Mrs. Eastborne was in the kitchen making a salad. Amanda was with her.

"Hi, Sara," Amanda said warmly. When she looked at Tim, her whole face lit up.

Sara's good mood began to deflate. So Amanda had stayed on after the tutoring session was over and Tim had left to pick Sara up at the dance studio. *She's probably hoping she'll be invited to dinner,* Sara thought bitterly.

"That smells great," Mrs. Eastborne said as she took the pizza box from Tim and set it on the table. "Getting pizza for dinner was an inspiration."

Sara felt a stab of impatience. Since when did picking up a pizza qualify as inspiration? When it was her turn to make supper, she went to the trouble of *cooking*.

"You're staying for dinner, I hope," Tim said to Amanda.

"We'd love to have you," Mrs. Eastborne added as she took several plates from the cupboard.

"Oh, I'd love to stay," Amanda said.

Sara didn't say anything at all.

When Tim left to drive Amanda home, Mrs. Eastborne went upstairs to take a bath and then to read in bed. Sara turned on the TV in the family room and stared blindly at the screen.

She had no idea what show she was watching when Tim came into the room twenty minutes later and gave her hair a playful tug.

"Why can't you keep away from my friends?"

she said coldly, continuing to stare blankly at the screen. "Why do you have to pick on Amanda, of all people?"

"Sari . . ."

"Don't," Sara snapped. "I'm not that dumb kid anymore, the one who believed everything you said!"

Tim sank into an easy chair and sighed deeply. "So, we're calling off the Great Pizza Parlor Peace Pact, huh?"

"Amanda didn't even ask me how dance class went!" Sara cried, her vision now blurry.

"Oh," Tim said quietly. "I get it. You're mad because you think I'm taking your best pal away. Well, you can relax, Sara. Amanda likes you, a *lot*. She says she's never had a better friend."

She won't feel that way for long, taunted a wicked little voice in a corner of Sara's mind.

"I want you to leave her alone," she said aloud. "There are plenty of other girls at Sweet Valley High you could go out with. You don't need Amanda."

"I *like* Amanda," Tim pointed out reasonably.

"You promised you wouldn't mess up my life!"

"But I didn't promise to be a hermit!" he replied angrily.

"Amanda wouldn't give you the time of day if she knew what you're really like," Sara said, and the moment the words were out of her mouth she regretted them. She really hadn't meant to be cruel.

Tim got up out of his chair and stood in front of Sara. "Oh?" he asked after a long, painful silence. "What *am* I really like, Sari? Why don't you tell me?"

Sara's throat was so tight that she couldn't have spoken even if she had wanted to. She got up and walked out of the room.

Tim followed her into the kitchen.

"Oh no you don't, Sari," he said with quiet determination. "This time you can't just cut me off, pretend I'm not here. I'm your brother, *your twin,* and that's reality. I'm not going anywhere, so you might as well start trying to accept me!"

"It was because of you," she whispered. "It was all because of you!"

"*What* was because of me?" Tim asked.

"The divorce," Sara said brokenly as she slammed both her fists down on the counter. "Mom and Dad broke up because of all the trouble you caused. That was why Dad moved out. He just couldn't handle it anymore!"

Tim paled, and his throat worked visibly as he swallowed. "Is that what you really think?" he asked evenly. "Where have you been for the last ten years, Sara? Living in some black-and-white sitcom? Mom and Dad were fighting *long* before I got into trouble the first time."

"That's not true," Sara said, shaking her head. "That's just not true." Sara pushed past Tim and started toward her room.

"Keep talking, Sara," Tim pleaded gruffly.

"Please don't walk away. We'll never be able to straighten things out between us if you do that."

Sara stopped and closed her eyes for a moment, but she didn't turn around. "I'm sorry," she said. "I can't. I just can't."

Sara washed her face, brushed her teeth, and changed into her favorite nightgown. Then she crawled into bed and lay there, staring at the ceiling. *Tim is right,* she thought, though she could never tell him so. She could hardly admit it to herself, let alone to her brother. *Mom and Dad's marriage had been in serious trouble even before Tim took his first drink.*

Sara dried her cheeks with the back of her hand and sniffled. She wanted more than anything to be mature about all this. So why was she acting like a hurt, angry little girl?

On Saturday morning, Jessica pulled the covers up over her head and groaned. "No, I'm not going to help you wash the car," she said, her voice muffled. "This is the first time in weeks I've been able to sleep in on a Saturday morning!"

Elizabeth smiled as the vacuum cleaner roared to life in the hallway outside the girls' rooms. "Give it up, Jess. Mom is on a housecleaning binge and Dad is pouring gas into the lawn mower even as we speak. It's going to get very *loud* around here."

"Noooooo," Jessica whined. "This is inhuman. It can't be any later than 6:30!"

"It's 10:45," Elizabeth replied.

Jessica sat up in bed, her hair all rumpled, her lower lip sticking out in a pout. "Nobody in this family cares about me at all!" she cried dramatically.

Elizabeth sighed. "I guess you're just going to have to report us for cheerleader abuse," she teased. "Or maybe it's beauty-queen bashing."

Jessica's blue-green eyes flashed with anger for a moment, but then she burst out laughing and flung her pillow at Elizabeth. "Where's your respect for royalty?" she demanded. "And why haven't you brought me breakfast in bed?"

"I'll bring you breakfast in bed, Your Highness, when pigs fly," Elizabeth replied sweetly as she picked up Jessica's pillow and threw it back at her.

Twenty minutes later, Jessica arrived in the kitchen, wearing white cut-offs and a pink polo shirt, her makeup flawless and her hair brushed to a glossy shine.

"Are you going to that shelter place today?" she asked Elizabeth as she took a banana from the fruit bowl in the center of the table and began to peel it.

Elizabeth shook her head. "No, but Enid and I are thinking about volunteering there on a regular basis. Abuse is a terrible problem, Jess, and it's growing."

Jessica shuddered, and then took a bite from her banana. "Why do women put up with being treated like that?" she asked after a moment. "I mean, can you picture Mom standing for it for one second?"

"No," Elizabeth admitted, "but Mom wasn't abused as a child, and she's a strong, confident woman with a solid career. Most battered women are carrying on a sort of tragic family tradition. They tolerate mistreatment because they think that's the way things are supposed to be. Most of the time they even believe they deserve to be hit."

Jessica's second bite of banana went down with a loud gulp. "*Nobody* deserves to be hit."

"You know that and I know that," Elizabeth said. "Now, if we could just let all those other girls and women out there in on the secret."

"I think you've been going to too many of those Triple A meetings," Jessica observed seriously. "You're beginning to sound like a visiting expert on *Donahue* or something."

Elizabeth laughed. "Triple A is an automobile club, Jess," she said when she had caught her breath. "You mean A.A., Alcoholics Anonymous."

Her sister looked miffed. "Well, it's not like everybody in the world *knows* that!"

That night Elizabeth went to the Beach Disco with Todd. Afterward they went to the Dairi Burger, and Jerry McAllister was there with his crowd. His purple van was parked in the spot closest to the building.

"Hi, Crunch," Todd said as he and Elizabeth passed the table. "Guys."

Jerry and his friends grunted some greetings.

"The roaring lion is a nice touch," Elizabeth said with a half-smile once she and Todd were seated in their regular booth.

"I would have expected him to go for a woman with snakes in her hair or something," Todd confided as he picked up the menu.

Elizabeth glanced out the window and saw a shadowy figure by Jerry's van. Then she recognized the person as Tim Eastborne.

He came in a few minutes later, grinning as though he had just seen something wondrous. Todd waved him over to their table.

"That is one great van out there," Tim said as he sat down.

"It belongs to Crunch McAllister," Todd explained. "And don't let him see you so much as breathe on it. He's pretty sensitive when it comes to that van."

Tim chuckled. "He didn't strike me as a really *sensitive* guy," Tim added.

"Are you alone tonight?" Elizabeth asked. She was surprised to see him without Amanda Hayes. In the past week the two of them had become something of an item at Sweet Valley High.

Tim nodded. "Amanda wants to get up early tomorrow and put in some practice time at the studio, so I took her home a few minutes ago."

Elizabeth glanced at the clock on the wall

behind the counter. It was 9:15. "How's Sara?"

"She's fine," Tim answered. "I think she and Bob went to a pool party at the country club tonight."

"Are things any better between the two of you?" Todd ventured. He and Tim had become friends over the past few days and Tim had told him as much about the painful situation with Sara as he could without breaking his promise to his sister.

"Not really," Tim replied. "But like those people I hang around with always say, things take time."

"I'm sure everything will work out," Elizabeth said earnestly.

The three of them ordered and they got into a lively discussion about Sweet Valley High's football season. Before Elizabeth knew it, it was eleven o'clock.

She yawned.

"Does this mean you want to go home?" Todd asked with a grin.

"Yes," Elizabeth answered. "It does."

"I'd better get home, too," Tim said. "I'm supposed to keep decent hours, and I don't want my mom to think I've strayed from the straight and narrow."

Todd paid the check, then he and Elizabeth and Tim left the Dairi Burger together. Jerry and his friends were still having a good time inside, and the parking lot was beginning to fill up with cars coming from the second shows at the movie theaters.

Tim said goodnight to Elizabeth and Todd, got into his mother's car, and drove off.

"He seems like such a nice guy," Todd remarked when he and Elizabeth were seated in his BMW.

"I suppose you've heard the rumors about him," Elizabeth said sadly.

"Reform school, drugs, alcohol," Todd answered. "Yeah, I heard. Do you think it's all true?"

"Maybe. But people change," she said. "And if they're trying to make things right, I think they deserve a second chance."

Todd nodded and let the subject drop. He didn't need to tear other kids down to feel good about himself, and that was another of the million and thirty-seven things Elizabeth liked about him.

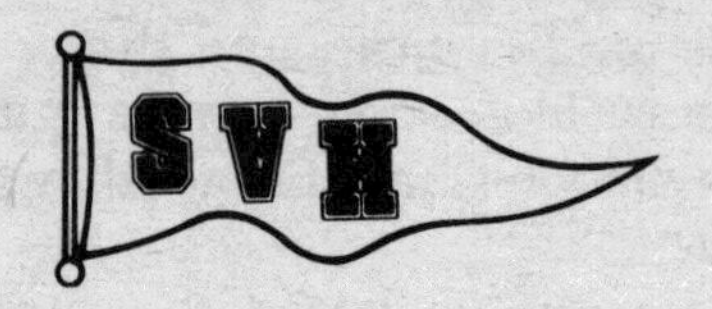

Seven

When Sara saw the police car pull up in front of the house early Sunday morning, her heart almost stopped beating. Even before the two officers came up the walk and rang the doorbell, she knew the worst was happening. Again.

Mrs. Eastborne must have seen the stricken expression on Sara's face as her daughter stood looking out the front window, since she already had her hand on the knob when the doorbell chimed.

Sara saw her mother flinch when she opened the door to find two policemen standing on the step.

"Yes?" she asked in a shaky voice.

"Is this the Eastborne residence?" inquired one of the officers.

Mrs. Eastborne nodded, all color draining from her face.

The other officer consulted a small notebook in his hand. "We're looking for a young man named Tim Eastborne. Would he be here, ma'am?"

"Yes," Mrs. Eastborne answered in a small voice. "He's here." She looked at her daughter, and Sara saw her mother's eyes haunted with old worries. At that moment, Sara hated Tim more than she ever had. "Get your brother, please," Mrs. Eastborne said.

Sara's shoulders were rigid as she walked through the house and knocked on Tim's bedroom door. He opened the door almost immediately. He had pulled on his jeans and shirt, but his hair was rumpled and Sara could tell he was still half asleep.

"The police are here to see you," she said. And then she turned and walked away. Part of her wanted to take refuge in her room until the whole terrible thing was over, but she couldn't bring herself to abandon her mother. Mrs. Eastborne needed someone to stand by her.

"A van was stolen from in front of the Dairi Burger last night," one of the policemen said to Tim when he entered the living room. "Witnesses report that you were seen loitering around the vehicle, and it disappeared about the time you left."

"I didn't take McAllister's van," Tim said. He sighed and ran his hand through his hair. "All I did was look at it."

"We'll have to take you in for some questioning, Mr. Eastborne," the other policeman said.

Mrs. Eastborne laid a hand on her chest. "Are you charging Tim with anything?"

"No, ma'am, not yet. But you might want to call your attorney."

"Just . . . just give us a few minutes, please," Mrs. Eastborne said. She walked over to a small table and searched through some papers for her address book.

Sara glared at Tim. When she caught his eye, he shook his head and looked away.

Mrs. Eastborne called her ex-husband in Connecticut first. Sara heard her leave a message on his answering machine. Next, she called her lawyer.

Sara's humiliation was even deeper then. The attorney's daughter was one of her friends at Sweet Valley High. A terrible headache began to pound under Sara's right temple.

"Yes, I'll meet you at the police station," Mrs. Eastborne said finally. Then she hung up the receiver and picked up her purse.

"Are you happy now?" Sara hissed at Tim as he walked past her to the front door.

Tim's jawline was hard, and his eyes snapped with anger, but he didn't answer her.

Sara stood at the window and watched as Tim was put into the back of the squad car. Mrs. Eastborne got in beside him.

All the neighbors are probably watching, Sara

thought grimly. So much for her big secret; it was Connecticut all over again.

About two hours later, Sara's mother and brother came home from the police station in a cab.

Tim went straight to his room and closed the door. Mrs. Eastborne came into the living room and brushed her hair back with both hands.

"Did your father call?" she asked.

Sara shook her head. She was surprised that her brother had been allowed to leave the police station. "What's going to happen to Tim?" she asked.

Mrs. Eastborne led the way into the kitchen, where she set about making herself a cup of tea. "I don't know. My lawyer says the police don't have enough evidence to hold him."

Sara put her arm around her mother's shoulders. "Is there anything I can do?"

"Yes," Mrs. Eastborne said, looking at Sara with pain-filled eyes. "You can believe in your brother. You can be on his side right now, when it counts."

Sara sighed and let her arm fall back to her side. "Mom, if a car was stolen and Tim was on the scene . . ."

Anger and frustration flared in Mrs. Eastborne's face, turning her cheeks bright pink. "Lots of other people were 'on the scene,'

Sara. Isn't it possible that one of *them* stole that van?"

"It's possible," Sara reflected, her voice soft with misery. "But Tim does have a record."

Tears shimmered along Mrs. Eastborne's lashes. "That doesn't make him guilty," she said. She took her cup of tea and returned to the living room.

Sara went to her mother's bedroom to get her her slippers. She saw the cord of the hallway phone running beneath Tim's door, and she could hear him talking to someone, his voice agitated and earnest. Her heart constricted painfully. She didn't *want* him to be guilty. She raised her hand to knock. Then she remembered Connecticut and walked on.

About half an hour later, a guy in jeans and a college sweatshirt arrived and asked to see Tim.

"Who's that?" Sara asked her mother after the visitor had disappeared into Tim's room.

"His name is Mike," Mrs. Eastborne answered distractedly. "I think he's Tim's A.A. sponsor. Why do you think your father hasn't called?"

"I don't know, Mom," she said sadly. She picked up Mrs. Eastborne's teacup and went back to the kitchen to refill it.

She was just returning with a fresh cup of tea when the telephone rang. Sara picked up the receiver, expecting to hear Amanda's voice, or maybe Bob's, accusing her of being a liar.

Instead, she heard her father say, "Hello, kitten. Is your mother there?"

Sara swallowed. "Yes, Dad. Just a second."

A moment later Mrs. Eastborne reached for the receiver eagerly.

"Yes," Sara heard her mother say. "Tim's home now. But he's not out of trouble, Jim. He could be taken into custody again at any time."

Sara closed her eyes and tuned out the conversation. She felt sick to her stomach. *If only Tim had stayed in Connecticut . . .*

Mike came out of Tim's room, nodded politely to Sara, and left.

Only when Mrs. Eastborne had finally hung up the phone did Tim join his mother and sister in the living room. He looked terrible, as though he hadn't slept in a week.

"I'm sorry," he said hoarsely.

You should be, Sara thought bitterly, but she couldn't bring herself to say the words aloud.

Mrs. Eastborne reached out to squeeze her son's hand. "Your dad is coming out on the next plane," she said. "He'll be here late tonight."

Surprise and happiness flickered in Tim's eyes. And then his shoulders slumped. "He probably just wants to tell me I'm an embarrassment to him," he said.

"He could have done that over the phone, without spending the time and money to fly out here," Mrs. Eastborne said kindly. Then she went into the kitchen to start lunch.

Sara went along to help, but mostly to avoid being alone in the same room with Tim.

Late that night, Mr. Eastborne pulled up in front of the house in a rented car. When he reached the front door he stood there awkwardly.

"Hello, Jim," Mrs. Eastborne finally said. "Come in."

"Hello, Janet." Mr. Eastborne looked at Tim and Sara with something like pain in his eyes. "Hi, kids."

Tim was standing by the couch, his arms folded, a defiant expression on his face. Sara knew he was bracing himself for an angry lecture from their father, and for a moment she felt bad for her brother.

"Have you eaten?" Mrs. Eastborne asked her ex-husband.

He nodded. "On the plane."

Same old Dad, Sara thought. *A real conversationalist.*

"I didn't steal the van, Dad," Tim said evenly.

To Sara's surprise, her father laid a hand on Tim's shoulder. "Let's talk about that," he said.

Mr. Eastborne sat down in a chair. Mrs. Eastborne settled at one end of the couch with Sara at the other. Tim remained standing, looking as though he might bolt for the door at any second.

"It's good to see you again, Janet," Mr. Eastborne said to his former wife. "You look great."

"Thank you," she said quietly.

Mr. Eastborne turned to look at Tim. "Now, tell me what happened."

Tim lifted his chin a notch or two. "I went to the movies with a friend last night," he said. "Amanda had to get up early for a dance lesson, so I took her straight home after the show. Then I went to the Dairi Burger to get something to eat." He perched on the arm of the sofa closest to his mother. "There was this really awesome van parked in the lot, so I stopped to check it out. Then I went inside and sat with some friends for a while, talking. I left when they did, came home, and went to bed. This morning the police showed up. The van had been stolen, and I'm the prime suspect."

"I wonder why," Sara murmured sarcastically. Tim stiffened slightly, as though he had been struck.

"Were any charges filed?"

"No," Mrs. Eastborne answered for her son. "There's no proof that Tim even touched that van."

Mr. Eastborne looked his son straight in the eye. "If you did take the van, son, we have to know about it. We can't help you if we don't know the truth."

Color flooded Tim's face. "All I did was look at it!" he cried. "I guess somebody should have told me that was a crime!"

"Take it easy, Tim," Mr. Eastborne instructed his son calmly.

Tim's shoulders slumped slightly, and he looked down at the carpet. "I swear it, Dad," he said. "I didn't take the van."

Sara wanted desperately to believe her brother, but she couldn't quite manage it. Tim had brought their mother's car home before eleven-thirty—their mother could testify to that—but that didn't mean he hadn't sneaked out again and gone back to the Dairi Burger to hot-wire Jerry McAllister's van. Tim knew a lot about engines, and she was sure her brother didn't need a key to start a motor.

"These friends you were with," Mr. Eastborne pressed. "Did they see you leave?"

Tim nodded. "Yes," he said. "But that's no proof that I didn't take the van. The police think I might have come back later."

Sara excused herself quietly and went to bed. She could hear her parents and her brother talking in the living room long after she had turned out the lights.

Monday morning, Sara was dreading getting up. She was sure that the account of the van theft would be in the first edition of the newspaper. And it might mention that Tim was taken in for questioning. She hoped they didn't have a picture of him at the police station in handcuffs.

For one desperate moment Sara thought about pretending to be sick so that she wouldn't have to go to school and face her friends. Then she rejected the idea. She knew no one would believe she was really ill.

Her mother and Tim were in the kitchen when she came down for breakfast. Mrs. Eastborne was dressed for work in an attractive blue suit and a lavender blouse. Tim was staring solemnly into a bowl of cold cereal.

Sara had expected her father to spend the night on the fold-out couch in the living room, but when she had come downstairs, there had been no sign of him. She felt a pang of disappointment. *He's probably already on the plane, heading back to his neat and tidy life in Connecticut,* she thought bitterly.

"Where's Dad?" she asked.

"Probably at his hotel," Mrs. Eastborne answered. She took a final sip of her coffee and consulted her watch. "Well, I'd better hurry if I'm going to catch the bus." She kissed Tim on top of the head and Sara on the cheek. "I'd like you to pick me up at work at five-fifteen," she said to her daughter, handing her the car keys.

Sara looked at her mother and then at the keys, but she didn't voice her confusion. First the news that her father was still in Sweet Valley, and now her mother's strange request. Life was getting far too messy.

"Are you going to give me a ride or do I have

to walk?" Tim asked Sara the moment the door had closed behind their mother.

"You mean, you're actually going to school?" *So that's why Mom gave me the keys! She wants to throw Tim and me together again!* she thought. She looked at her brother in disbelief.

Tim nodded grimly. "Sure I am. If I don't, everybody will say that I couldn't face the other kids because I'm guilty. And I'm not."

Sara's cheeks burned, and she averted her eyes for a moment. She wanted to believe Tim more than she had ever wanted anything before, but she was just too terrified of being let down again. Trusting someone just hurt *too much.*

Tim surprised her by reaching out and squeezing her hand briefly. "I know it's tough being my sister," he said with a half-smile. "I also know that the last thing you want is advice from me, but I've got to say this, Sari. You'd feel better if you'd go to Alateen and talk to the other kids about having an alcoholic for a brother."

Sara's eyes began to sting again. She had never cried as much in her entire life as she had since Tim's arrival in Sweet Valley. She pulled her hand away. "I don't need meetings. There's nothing wrong with me."

"Sara." Tim sighed. "You've lied to all your friends. You built me up into something I never was, and now your life is collapsing because you just won't trust or believe in anyone. Does that sound like normal stuff to you?"

"I wouldn't have had to lie if it hadn't been for you!" she cried angrily. "Sometimes I really hate you!"

"I guess this means I'll be walking to school," Tim replied after a long, tense silence.

Sara didn't answer her brother. She didn't even look at Tim again. But she did wait until he was in the car with her before driving off.

Jerry McAllister and a group of his friends were waiting for them when Sara brought the car to a stop in the parking lot at Sweet Valley High. She felt her stomach tighten with fear.

"It's OK," Tim told her as he opened his door. "Just don't get out of the car until you're sure it's safe."

In spite of her own feelings of anger toward her brother, Sara was terrified. "Tim, don't . . ."

The car door closed, and Sara had no idea whether Tim had heard her or not. She laid her forehead against the steering wheel for a moment, her heart pounding with terror, then looked up to see Todd Wilkins and some of his friends gravitating toward the scene. She felt a rush of gratitude when they grouped themselves around Tim.

Tim is brave, Sara reflected as she watched through the windshield. *Either that, or he's crazy.* She pushed open the door and got out.

"Where's my van, Eastborne?" Jerry demanded loudly as he pushed himself away from the fender of the sports car he had been leaning against.

"I couldn't tell you," Tim answered evenly. He stood straight and tall and looked Jerry square in the eye.

He's got to know Jerry could mop the ground with him if he wanted, Sara thought as she watched her brother defend himself.

"I haven't seen it since Saturday night," Tim added.

"Neither have I," Jerry replied. His friends laughed as though he had made a witty remark. And then, when Tim was off guard, Jerry threw a punch that sent Tim stumbling backward.

Sara covered her mouth with both hands and swallowed a scream. Blood was trickling from Tim's lip, and it looked as if there was going to be a brawl right there in the school's parking lot.

"Stay back," Tim said to Todd and the others, glaring now at Jerry. "This is my fight."

After what seemed to Sara like ages, but what was probably only a minute, Mr. Collins and two other teachers came running across the lot and, with some help from Todd, Tony Esteban, Ken Matthews, and Tom McKay, managed to pull Jerry and Tim apart.

"You," Mr. Collins told Jerry sternly. "Knock it off right now! And get off this campus." He turned to look at Tim, who was breathing hard and wiping his bloody mouth with the back of his hand. "I'll see you in the office."

Sara felt relieved that the fight was over and that Tim hadn't been seriously hurt, but she knew that now her brother was in even deeper trouble than before. He would probably be suspended from school before the day was over.

History is definitely repeating itself, Sara thought, and she almost laughed at the tragic nature of her family's life. Wildly, she wished the ground would open up and swallow her, like in one of those stupid horror movies.

But it didn't, and Sara had to go inside just as if nothing unusual had happened. The first person she met in the hall was Amanda.

There was no reason to wonder whether or not Amanda had heard the news about Tim. She glared at Sara and said, "You could have told me what to expect."

Sara didn't know how to answer her friend. She might have tried to explain that she had been too afraid to tell Amanda about Tim because of what had happened back in Connecticut. It was the truth, after all. She *had* been afraid. But for some reason now, her fear and distrust seemed like pretty weak reasons for having deceived her best friend.

When Sara continued in her silence, Amanda whirled on her heel and walked away.

"Sara?"

Sara turned at the sound of the soft, sympathetic voice, and saw Elizabeth Wakefield standing there.

"I know Tim didn't steal Jerry's van," Elizabeth said. "Todd and I both saw him leave."

Sara couldn't say anything. All she could do

was hope desperately that, by some miracle, Elizabeth was right.

Elizabeth touched her arm. "If you need to talk to somebody," she said, "let me know." And then she was gone.

Throughout her first class, Sara remained in a daze. She almost decided to leave California for good, to go someplace where no one knew her, someplace where she could be a stranger, where she could start life all over again.

Then, as if she were holding up a mental mirror, she suddenly saw that her crazy idea of running away from her problems came from self-pity. She was feeling sorry for herself. And only cowards did that.

She remembered how Tim had faced Jerry McAllister in the parking lot that morning. Her brother had shown a lot of courage in coming to Sweet Valley, too. Maybe he didn't always display the best judgment, but nobody could say that Tim Eastborne wasn't brave.

No, Sara thought glumly, *I'm the coward in the Eastborne family, not Tim.* He had been willing to face the accusations, the inevitable snide remarks and glances, the rejection. For the first time since the police had come to the door Sunday morning, it occurred to Sara that Tim might—just *might*—really be innocent.

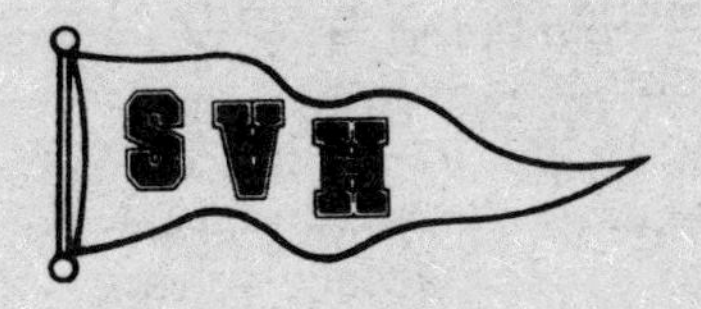

Eight

Tim had been sent home from school because of the fight with Jerry McAllister and, when Sara arrived later that afternoon, he was sitting in the living room with Mr. Eastborne. His lip was swollen and his eyes still had that defiant, I'll-stand-my-ground-no-matter-what look in them.

"Tough day, sweetheart?" Mr. Eastborne asked. He stood up and put his arms around her.

Sara nodded and let her forehead rest against his chest. Why not pretend, just for a moment, that she had a real father, just as she had pretended she had a brother back in the pizza place the other day?

Finally, Sara stepped away from Mr. Eastborne and sat down.

The newspaper was lying on the coffee table. Sweet Valley was a relatively small town, where not much happened in the way of crime. Just as Sara had suspected, the stolen-van incident was reported on the front page.

Sara covered her face with both hands.

"I wish I'd never come here," Tim said in a voice so low it was barely audible.

That makes two of us, Sara thought.

"I think we should all go out to dinner tonight," Mr. Eastborne said a little too heartily. "What do you say? We'll pick your mother up at her office and then have seafood at the best restaurant in town."

Sara lowered her hands, about to protest that she didn't feel like going out and facing Sweet Valley again after the day she had had, but something about the depressed look on Tim's face stopped her.

"OK," Sara heard herself say. "Seafood sounds like a good idea to me, and Mom really likes it."

Mrs. Eastborne was pleasantly surprised when her former husband and her children picked her up at the office. Tim and Sara sat quietly in the back seat, very careful not to look at each other.

During dinner at the Shore House, a fancy new restaurant overlooking the beach, Sara's throat kept tightening up. *This is how it should have been,* she thought, as her father laughed at one of Tim's corny jokes. *This is the sort of family we could have been.*

Once again she felt angry, but this time she wasn't sure just who she was angry with. This time it wasn't quite so easy to place all the blame on Tim.

"Come in and have coffee?" Mrs. Eastborne invited when Mr. Eastborne parked his rental car in the driveway later that night.

Sara's father rubbed his chin thoughtfully. "I'd like that, Janet," he said. "But the truth is, well, I need to talk over a few more things with Tim." He glanced briefly at his son, then faced his ex-wife again. "Would that be all right?"

Mrs. Eastborne nodded and got out of the car, and Sara followed. Tim slid into the front seat without saying a word.

When Sara and her mother had gone inside the house, Mr. Eastborne drove away.

Sara gathered up all her courage and asked, "Are you and Dad thinking about getting back together?"

Mrs. Eastborne's weary eyes darted to Sara's face. "Oh, honey, no. Did we give you that impression? Your father has his life on the East Coast, and I have mine here. He just came out to California because you and Tim needed him."

Sara couldn't hide her skeptical expression; it was just there all of a sudden, taking up her whole face. "He never cared before whether or not we needed him," she said.

Her mother sank into a chair with a sigh.

"Some people change, Sara. And your dad is trying to establish some kind of communication with you and Tim. Please don't shut him out."

The doorbell rang before Sara could think of a reply, and she hurried off to answer it.

Bob was standing on the step, looking grim and holding that day's edition of the *Sweet Valley News*. "Could I talk to you for a minute?" he asked stiffly, as though Sara were a stranger and they had never kissed or danced or dreamed together.

A feeling of dread crowded her throat, but Sara managed to smile. "Sure. Come in."

Bob eyed the house uneasily. "Maybe we could just sit in my car."

Sara told her mother she would be back in a little while and followed Bob down the walk. When they were seated in the vehicle's cushy leather interior, Bob refused to look at her. He simply tossed the folded newspaper into her lap.

"Bob, what's this all about?" she asked. *Of course, I know what this is about,* she added silently.

His hands tightened on the steering wheel. "I don't think we should see each other for a while," he said.

Sara closed her eyes for a moment. Bob's words had struck her dumb even though she had expected him to say exactly what he had. "Because of Tim?"

"My dad is an important man in this town,"

Bob said. "I have to think about how things look."

Sara wanted so much to cry, but her pride wouldn't allow it. She would shed the tears later, when she was alone and no one could see. "Bob," she said after she had regained her composure, "*I* didn't get taken in for questioning. My brother did."

"That's almost as bad," Bob sputtered, obviously anxious to be done with breaking up and to get out of there. For all Sara knew, he had a date with another girl, one who came from a more respectable family.

Sara wanted to hit him, but she just opened the car door and got out. "Goodbye," she said with all the dignity she could manage. The tears were very close now.

"I'll need my letterman's jacket back," Bob said from the shadowy interior of the car.

"No problem," Sara answered. *It's a good thing I don't have to cross the street to get back to the house,* she thought as her tears began to flow. *I can hardly see.*

"Sara?" Mrs. Eastborne called anxiously when her daughter came in.

Sara looked in the living room and just shook her head, silently telling her mother she couldn't talk. Then she went straight through the house to the backyard and sat in the old tire swing the last owners had left behind. For a very long time she spun around and around in the darkness.

* * *

Tim came home about an hour later. Mr. Eastborne had driven off without coming into the house. By then, Sara was stretched out on the family room couch, staring blindly at the TV screen, just as she had the other night.

"Hi, Sari," Tim said quietly. "Where's Mom?"

"In her room," Sara answered, keeping her eyes on the TV screen. "She has a headache."

"I guess that's no wonder," Tim said ruefully as he sank into a chair. "I'm sorry you've had such a hell of a day."

"You don't know the half of it," Sara said, her tone expressionless, her face wooden. She refused to look at Tim. Any trace of understanding or trust she may have felt at dinner had been wiped out by the confrontation with her boyfriend. "Bob and I broke up tonight. It seems he doesn't want to associate with the criminal element."

Tim's sigh was sharp and ragged. "That idiot. He shouldn't blame you for my problems."

Sara shrugged. "He won't be the only one who walks out on us. You don't see Amanda hanging around here, do you?"

Decisively, Tim reached for the telephone on the end table. "And on that note, it's time I called her and found out where we stand."

"I don't know where she stands," Sara said in the same spiritless monotone, "but I'm pretty sure you and I are out in the proverbial cold."

"Hello," Tim said a moment later. "This is Tim Eastborne. Is Amanda there, please?"

He waited and so did Sara. She was glad he couldn't know she was holding her breath.

"I see," he said finally, and the two words rang with disappointment. "No, that's OK. Thanks. Goodnight, Mrs. Hayes."

Tim hung up the receiver. Out of the corner of her eye, Sara saw that he was staring at the TV screen as vacantly as she had been.

"Wasn't she home?" Sara asked.

"She was there," Tim answered, the light from the screen flickering weirdly over his face. "She just didn't want to talk to me. Maybe she and Bob should get together."

Sara didn't appreciate the grim humor of her brother's remark. She missed Amanda desperately, and, in spite of Bob's behavior earlier that evening, she knew she would miss him, too. "What did Dad want to talk to you about?" she asked coldly.

"He offered to take me back to Connecticut with him, provided we can work out an agreement with the police."

"For good?"

"Yeah," Tim said. "I guess you'd like that, wouldn't you?"

Sara wanted to cry again, but she had

no more tears left. She shrugged and kept her eyes pointed at the TV screen as Tim left the room.

Tuesday at lunchtime, Sara decided to sit with Amanda. Her fear of being rejected was so acute, it made a sound like a dull roar in her ears. But she had learned one thing from the way Tim had stood up to Jerry McAllister in the parking lot. Sometimes, a person just had to face a difficult situation straight on.

"Hi, Amanda," she said softly.

Amanda looked up at her, then turned her eyes away. "Hi," she said reluctantly.

Sara was grateful that they were alone at the table, and that Tim was nowhere in sight. Maybe he had brought lunch from home and gone off somewhere by himself.

"I'm really sorry I didn't tell you about Tim," Sara said.

A tear trickled down Amanda's cheek, but she shrugged. "Hey, no problem," she said. "I guess I was pretty naive, thinking best friends should trust each other enough to share everything important."

Sara ran her tongue over dry lips. "I was too scared to tell you," she said in a small voice. "I was afraid you wouldn't like me anymore, because of Tim."

Amanda's eyes flashed with anger and hurt.

"I'm not mad at you because of what Tim did, Sara," she said. "I'm mad because you didn't think you could trust me!"

"I was wrong, Amanda, I'm not denying that. If you don't want to be friends anymore, I understand. What I don't understand is why you wouldn't even let Tim explain things to you on the telephone last night."

"He lied to me, too. Or, at least, he left the truth out of everything he said."

"He *wanted* to be honest with you, Amanda. Tim really likes you a lot. But I asked him not to tell you about what went on in Connecticut because I was ashamed."

Amanda sat quietly for a moment. Then she stood and picked up her tray. "Excuse me. I'm not very hungry anymore," she said before walking away.

She had not been gone more than a moment or two when Elizabeth Wakefield approached the table and sat down where Amanda had been. There was understanding in her blue-green eyes, and Sara was grateful that Elizabeth was willing to show her support of Tim so publicly.

"You know, I'm doing a series of articles for *The Oracle* on some of the organizations and programs that work from the community center," Elizabeth said. "I'm dropping by an Alateen meeting after school. Want to go with me?"

Sara felt all broken inside. *Elizabeth is probably*

the last friend I have left, she thought. "OK," she said quietly. "I'll go."

After the last bell, Elizabeth met Sara at her locker. They walked together to the parking lot and got into Elizabeth's car.

"Why are you doing this?" Sara finally asked when they were pulling out of the school parking lot. "Why aren't you ignoring me, like the rest of the kids are?"

"They're not ignoring you, Sara," Elizabeth said. "It's just that they don't know how to get past that wall you've put around yourself."

Sara tried to talk, but no words came out.

"It's hard to know what to say to someone who's so upset," Elizabeth went on. "Most kids aren't willing to risk it."

Sara looked out the passenger window and thought about what Elizabeth had just said. She had never looked at things that way before. Not here in Sweet Valley, and not back in Connecticut, either. Was it possible that Darlene and the others had *wanted* to reach out to her, but that she had put them off with her anger and her hurt and her shame? It was too late to change anything about those days. But maybe it wasn't too late to change something about *today*.

The Alateen meeting was held in the basement of the community center. Though she tried to pay attention, Sara didn't get a whole lot out of the meeting. She just couldn't concentrate. Her mind was spinning with possibilities she had never considered before.

At the end of the meeting, she took a printed schedule of the times and places the different Alateen groups met.

"I don't remember a thing anybody said," Sara confessed when she and Elizabeth were back in the Fiat again.

Elizabeth smiled. "From what some of the participants have told me, it takes time," she replied. "You just keep going back, and going back, and going back. Somehow, eventually, it all sinks in."

As Elizabeth drove, Sara thought of Tim and how he went so faithfully to his A.A. meetings, read his literature, and talked to his sponsor. Maybe he had stolen Jerry's van, and maybe he hadn't, but there was one thing Sara knew for certain: Even though these were probably some of the toughest days of his life, Tim hadn't had to drink in order to cope.

"Liz, what am I going to do?" Sara asked miserably when her friend brought the Fiat to a stop in front of the Eastborne house. "I don't want to be alone again."

"Try reaching out to people, Sara. Let them know how you feel."

"I did try," Sara protested. "Today, in the cafeteria, with Amanda. You probably saw what happened. She walked away from me."

"She's angry and hurt right now," Elizabeth said. "She'll work it through in her own time."

Sara managed a smile, which seemed like a miracle because she felt as if the world had ended. "How did you get to be so smart?"

Elizabeth laughed. "I'm a quick study. I have to confess I learned everything I told you tonight from the different twelve-step groups I've attended recently.

"Thanks, Liz," Sara said as she opened the door of the Fiat and got out. "I really appreciate the way you've stood by Tim and me."

Elizabeth smiled. "That's what friends are for. See you at school tomorrow."

When Sara got inside the house, she was surprised to find that her father was there, alone. And she was alarmed.

"Is something wrong?" she blurted out, feeling the color drain from her face. Maybe Tim had been taken to jail again, or her mother had had an accident on the freeway, or had gotten sick. . . .

"No, sweetheart," Mr. Eastborne said quickly. He came over to kiss her forehead. "I just wanted some private time with you, like I had with Tim the other night. That's OK, isn't it?"

"Sure," she said, trying to sound nonchalant though her heart was beating furiously. "I guess you'll be leaving soon, going back to Connecticut."

Mr. Eastborne nodded. "My in basket at the office is probably piled to the ceiling by now," he said. "But right now, my work isn't what matters. I want to talk about *you*, Sara."

"Tim said he might go back to live with you again, if the police let him leave the state."

Her father grinned. "I don't want to talk about Tim, either. Let's go and take a walk along the beach."

Sara nodded.

The beach wasn't crowded this late in the afternoon, and Sara and her father walked along the shore in silence. After a while they sat down on a wooden bench.

"I know you like it here in Sweet Valley," her father said. His eyes were fixed on the purple and pink horizon. "Your mother tells me you're pretty happy."

I was happy, Sara thought. "It's nice here," she said lamely.

"I'd like it a lot if you'd come back to Connecticut to visit for a few weeks next summer. Maybe we could go to New York and see a show."

Sara looked down at her hands, clenched in her lap. "You'd have time for that?" she asked, tears threatening to fall for what must have been the millionth time in the past few days.

Mr. Eastborne took his daughter's hand and squeezed it. "I'll *make* time," he promised gruffly.

Sara didn't try to pull her hand away. She sat there, waiting for what he had to say next.

"I know I haven't always shown it, kitten,"

Mr. Eastborne continued after a moment, "but I love you and your brother very much. I'd like to have a second chance with you, if you'll let me."

How many times had Sara fantasized about her father telling her that he loved her? Now it was actually happening, her dad was actually reaching out to her, and Sara didn't know quite how to respond.

"I love you, too, Dad," she said softly.

Mr. Eastborne put his arm around Sara's shoulders and pulled her close. "I know things look pretty bleak to you now, honey, but it's all going to work out."

Sara smiled through her tears. Having her father hold her close and reassure her felt so good it almost made up for the fact that he was probably completely wrong about things working out.

After a few minutes, Sara and Mr. Eastborne left the bench and started to walk down the beach again. They stopped to buy hot dogs for dinner. It wasn't until the sun went down that they went back to the car.

When he brought the car to a stop in front of Sara's house, Mr. Eastborne leaned over and kissed her on the temple. "I'll see you again before I leave," he promised, and the words nestled against Sara's heart.

Sara went inside the house, feeling as though some disjointed part of her spirit had finally been put back in place.

"Hi," her mother greeted her. Mrs. Eastborne had been watching the evening news in the living room. "Had dinner?"

Sara nodded. "Dad and I had hot dogs on the beach. He wants me to visit him next summer. What do you suppose has come over him?"

Mrs. Eastborne chuckled and muted the TV sound by pressing a button on the remote. "Maybe he finally realized that life isn't a dress rehearsal. This is the whole show, and what we waste is gone forever."

"Yeah," Sara agreed. "I never thought he'd change, though. Did you?"

"Actually, no," Mrs. Eastborne admitted. "But I'm glad he did. And there's another lesson here, Sara. Maybe your dad isn't the only Eastborne who's turned over a new leaf."

Sara drew a deep breath and let it out slowly. "Is Tim around?"

Mrs. Eastborne shook her head. "He's gone to a meeting with Mike."

I'm so glad Tim has Mike for a friend, Sara thought. *And Elizabeth and Todd. They really stood by him, even when I didn't.*

Sara considered going to her room to do her homework, but that night she wanted to be close to another person. The world didn't seem so big and dark and threatening when someone else was nearby.

"Mind if I join you down here?" Sara asked her mother.

Mrs. Eastborne pressed the remote button, and Dan Rather's voice was audible again. "Dan and I would consider it an honor."

Sara spread her books out on the coffee table, got a soda from the kitchen, and settled down to work. As she sat there in the warm light of the living room lamps, she thought how lucky she was to really *belong* somewhere.

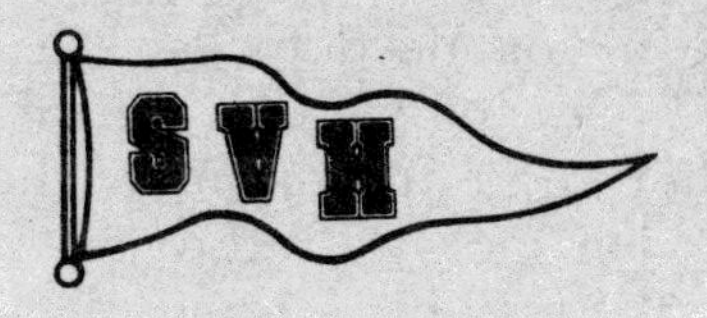

Nine

"It's an awful time to have to leave town on business," Mrs. Eastborne apologized on Wednesday afternoon. Sara had come home from school to find her mother packing. "I'm afraid it can't be helped, though. This is a big account and the company's third-quarter profits might depend on my landing the job."

Sara sat in the chintz-covered armchair in her mother's room. "I understand, Mom," she said. "Don't worry. Tim and I will be perfectly fine here by ourselves."

It seemed to Sara that her mother's shoulders stiffened slightly at the mention of Tim, but then she decided she must have been imagining things. If anything new was going on with the police investigation, her mother would have told her.

"I'll call as soon as I've checked into my hotel," Mrs. Eastborne said, sounding rushed and a little frazzled. "I'll be at the Sheraton in Sacramento if you need to leave a message." She handed Sara the keys to her car. "Now, if you wouldn't mind driving me to the airport?"

Sara took her mother to the airport and saw her off. On the way back home, she passed the community center and recognized some kids from the Alateen meeting she had attended with Elizabeth. They were sitting in a big circle on the center's lawn.

On impulse, Sara stopped, parked the car, and joined the others.

"Hi, Sara," whispered a familiar-looking girl with blond hair and braces. She moved over to make a space in their circle. "It's such a nice day, we decided to have the meeting out here."

Sara nodded. She wrapped her arms around her updrawn knees and turned her attention to the boy who was talking. At the first meeting, Sara hadn't taken in much of anything, but at this one, she was like a sponge.

By the time the meeting was over and Sara was walking back to the car, she had come to terms with a few things. Tim's problems were strictly his own, she realized, but how *she* reacted to them was her own responsibility. She had choices. She didn't have to let the things other people did rule her life.

Sara arrived home to find a note from Tim stuck to the refrigerator door with a magnet. It said he had gone to a meeting.

Sara was anxious to talk to her brother, to tell him she believed in him now. She hoped with all her heart that she and Tim could find some common ground and be friends again, as they had been when they were kids.

Knowing Tim loved chili, Sara lined up the ingredients on the breakfast bar and began to cook. The pot of savory beans and meat was bubbling away on the stove when there was a knock at the back door.

Sara looked up and saw her father on the other side of the glass, and she hurried over to let him in. Since their evening together, she had also been thinking about some of her attitudes toward Mr. Eastborne, and how it might be best if she changed them.

"Hi," she said. "I'm making chili for supper. Can you stay?"

Mr. Eastborne shook his head. "I'm sorry, sweetheart, but no. I have something important to tell you, then I'm off to the airport to catch my plane home."

Sara felt sad to think of her father leaving, even though she had known this moment would come. She felt a tickle of uneasiness in the pit of her stomach.

Mr. Eastborne took a seat at the table and Sara made him a quick cup of coffee in the microwave, then joined him.

"What is it?" she asked nervously.

Mr. Eastborne smiled. "I just came from the police station, and I have very good news. They've located the McAllister van, and the fingerprints they found inside belong to a suspected car thief from the next town. They've already made an arrest and, of course, Tim is cleared of all suspicion in the matter."

Sara wanted to jump up and shout for joy, but she also felt no small amount of shame for the way she had treated her brother earlier. "Oh, Dad, that's great!"

"Is your mother around?" Mr. Eastborne asked. "I'd like to tell her, too."

"Mom had to leave town on business," Sara said. "I'll call her at the hotel tonight and let her know."

"Fine." Mr. Eastborne cleared his throat and shifted uncomfortably in his chair. "There's something else, Sara, and I'll admit I'm pretty nervous about how you're going to take it."

Sara's eyebrows drew together in a frown. "What is it?"

"I've met a woman, back in Connecticut. Her name is Genna Bates and, well, I'm thinking of marrying her."

A whole cyclone of mixed emotions spun inside Sara as she tried to absorb this news. And then, strangely, she was calm. "I'm happy for you, Dad," she said sincerely.

"Now, you remember," Mr. Eastborne said as he rose from his chair. "I'm counting on you to come visit me for a couple of weeks next summer."

"I'll remember," Sara said softly. "I love you, Dad. And thanks for the great news."

After her father had gone, Sara was even more anxious to talk with Tim. She wanted so much to straighten things out between them, once and for all.

Finally, when the chili was done and had long since been turned down to simmer, and there was still no sign of Tim, Sara began to get worried.

She decided to read a bit to calm her impatience and anxiety. When she went to her room for a book, she spotted an envelope lying on her pillow. *Sari* was written on the front in Tim's strong, square handwriting.

A feeling of dread came over Sara as she reached for the envelope, opened it, and sank onto her bed to read the single sheet inside.

Dear Sari,

I guess I'm a coward for saying goodbye to you this way, instead of face-to-face. The plain truth is, I didn't want to see how happy you would be to get rid of me.

By now, Dad has probably told you that I've been cleared of stealing Jerry McAllister's van, which is why I'm allowed to leave the state. I'm going back to Connecticut, Sari. I don't really want to live with Dad and his girlfriend, so I'll be going to a boarding school upstate. Thanks to my experience at Rivercrest, I can deal with the concept of living at school.

I'm sure your life will be much simpler, and much happier, now that I'm gone for good. Mom knows about the decision, but I asked her not to tell you because I wanted you to find out from me, even indirectly.

The kids at school will forget about me soon, and things will return to normal, I promise. Take care, and good luck.

Love, Tim

Sara crumpled the page in her hand and let it fall to the floor of her room. Then she hurried down the hall to Tim's room and threw the door open.

She checked the closet, then the dresser drawers, panic rising inside her as she realized that it was no joke. Tim really was going back to Connecticut, and he was doing it because he thought that was what Sara wanted. She knew it was his way of making up for the trouble he had caused her.

Sarra suddenly realized that her father must have known about Tim's decision when he came by earlier. Tim may have been waiting in his car the whole time Sara and Mr. Eastborne were talking in the kitchen. Tim had probably asked him not to tell her anything, just as he had asked their mother to keep his decision a secret.

Wildly, Sara searched her mind for the name of her father's airline. When she remembered, she called the airport and asked if a Tim Eastborne was booked on the next flight to Hartford, Connecticut.

"Yes, he is," the clerk said after consulting her computer. "Did you want to give Mr. Eastborne some message?"

"Yes!" Sara blurted. "Tell him not to get on that plane!" She stretched the phone cord to its limit so she could turn off the stove and snatch up the car keys.

"I'm afraid I can't do that," the clerk responded politely. "Is this some sort of joke?"

Sara groaned in frustration and hung up. She could have had Tim paged, and have him call home, but she couldn't just stand there and wait for his call. She had to *do* something.

Sara ran out to the car, started the engine, and raced through Sweet Valley and out onto the freeway.

By the time she finally reached the concourse, Tim and her father's flight number was being called. Breathless, Sara scanned the passengers waiting to board.

And then she spotted Tim, standing next to his father but staring wistfully out through the big windows at the aircraft that would carry him away from Sweet Valley, his mother, his sister, and Amanda.

"Tim?"

Tim turned and looked at his sister in surprise. Sara noticed that their father was smiling. He winked at her and walked over to wait in line with the other passengers.

"What are you doing here?" Tim demanded.

"I need a second chance, Tim. I was unfair

to you, I let you down, and I'm sorry. If you'll just come home with me . . ."

"Home?" Tim laughed bitterly and shook his head. "You mean that place where everybody is supposed to believe in you? I don't think I have one of those, Sara."

Sara sighed. "This is no time to dig your heels in and act stubborn, Tim Eastborne. Mom and I love you."

"Are you asking me to come back to ease your conscience? Because you believed all along that I was guilty of stealing Jerry's van?"

"Partly," Sara admitted. She thought it was high time for some of that honesty they had talked about at Alateen. "I'm not a perfect sister, all right? You're not a perfect brother, either, in case you've forgotten." She paused and rested her hands on her hips. "But I'd like a chance to work on being a *better* sister, and I can't very well do that if you're on the other side of the country!"

Tim shoved a hand through his hair. "Do you really mean what you're saying, or are you going to get on my case about all the mistakes I've made in the past as soon as that plane takes off without me?"

"I really mean it," Sara said softly. She had finally gotten the old Tim back, and she was not going to let him go without a fight. "Come on, let's say goodbye to Dad and go home. I made chili for dinner."

"And cornbread?" Tim asked.

Sara shook her head and laughed. "No. But there's a mix in the cupboard," she said.

Tim and Sara turned toward their father just in time to see him grin, wave goodbye, and disappear down the jetway. Then they went to the airline counter and arranged for Tim's luggage to be sent back to Sweet Valley. When they turned away from the counter, Tim held out his hand.

"Keys," he ordered.

Sara pretended to glare at him. "I beg your pardon?"

They started to walk along the concourse, toward the parking area. "I want to drive," he said.

"We all want things, brother dear," Sara answered sweetly. "That doesn't mean we always get them. Why should I hand over the car keys to you, anyway?"

"Because I'm the guy, that's why."

"I should have let you get on that plane with Dad!" Sara retorted. "What a chauvinist!"

Tim shrugged. "Well, I tried."

When they got home, Sara put a pan of cornbread into the oven to bake and turned the burner on under the chili to warm it. While Sara was busy in the kitchen, Tim dialed the number of his mother's hotel in Sacramento and asked for Janet Eastborne's room.

"Hi, Mom," he said after a few moments of waiting.

Sara smiled. *Mom will be so happy when she*

finds out Tim is staying in Sweet Valley, Sara thought as she watched her brother.

"No, I'm not calling from the plane," he said. "I'm in the kitchen, where Sari is about to poison me with her famous chili. . . . Yeah, well, we're going to try to negotiate some kind of peace. . . . Right. . . . OK, I'll tell her. Bye, Mom. See you when you get home."

He hung up the telephone and went to the refrigerator for some milk. After pouring a glass, he turned to Sara and said, "Mom says she loves you, and that you're supposed to let *me* drive the whole time she's gone."

Sara laughed. "I'll buy the first part," she replied, "but you're not getting the car keys away from me with a flimsy line like that."

Tim sighed again. "You know," he said, "I think I might be losing my touch."

"For conning people? Don't look now, Tim, but that *might* be a good thing."

Tim went to the cupboard for dishes and glasses. "What made you change your mind, Sari? As recently as yesterday, you couldn't wait to get rid of me."

"I went to an Alateen meeting with Elizabeth Wakefield the other day after school, and to tell you the truth, I didn't take in much at the time. But today I went to another one, and it really got me thinking. I have a long way to go, Tim, but I know that I need to stop trying to run your life and concentrate on managing my *own,* which, at the moment, is pretty messy."

Tim carried the pot of chili to the table and

set it down on a potholder, then he and Sara sat down to eat.

"You had a good reason to be mad at me," Tim said after they had both filled their bowls with steaming chili. "But I'm glad you've decided to bury the hatchet. Hey, have you thought about where you'll be going to college?"

"UCLA, I think," Sara answered. She felt warm and good and lucky again. True, she had lost Bob, and that would hurt for a while. Things were all wrong between her and Amanda, too. But maybe if she and Tim could establish peaceful communications, there would be a chance of making things right with her best friend. "What about you?"

Tim finished buttering a chunk of cornbread. "It's vocational school for me," he said. "I haven't decided whether to go into computers or car repair yet."

"Maybe you could do both," Sara said excitedly. "Aren't a lot of engine problems diagnosed by computer these days?"

Tim nodded, his eyes alight with enthusiasm. He started to talk about clogged carburetors and federal emission standards, and Sara listened attentively, though she didn't understand a word.

"What about Amanda?" Sara asked when their meal was over and they had rinsed the dishes and cleaned up the kitchen. "Are you going to go and talk things through with her?"

"Probably not," Tim said sadly. "I don't

think I can take another rejection from her. Besides, Amanda's headed for college, like you. What does a girl like that have in common with a guy like me?"

"Hey," Sara protested. "I remember how you two looked at each other. It was pure poetry. You two were crazy about each other."

Tim nodded. "And I'm still crazy about her," he confessed. "Trouble is, the feeling isn't mutual."

"How do you know?"

"I know," Tim said, and Sara could tell by his tone that the subject was closed.

Elizabeth typed the last few words of her article, pushed back her chair, and sighed. "Done," she said.

Penny Ayala raised her eyes from the paste-ups she had been going over and smiled.

"If it was anyone else, I'd wait until I read the piece to offer my congratulations on a job well done, but because it's *you*, I'll congratulate you now. The article is sensitive, insightful, and just plain fabulous."

Elizabeth's smile was a little thin and a lot weary when she faced Penny. "I think I'd like to work on something a little lighter next time."

Penny left her chair to come and perch on the edge of Elizabeth's desk. "It really got you down, didn't it? Seeing all those women who'd been abused, working with their kids. Then going to those self-help sessions *and* the A.A. meetings!"

Elizabeth nodded. "I tried to be detached, like a good reporter is supposed to be, but my heart kept throwing itself right into the middle of the situations, and I found myself hurting right along with everyone else."

"You've got compassion for people, Liz," Penny told her friend. "That's why your writing is so good. Would you be willing to trade that human quality for something like perfect punctuation?"

"I guess not." Elizabeth sighed. The school was quiet except for the sound of the janitor's broom thumping against lockers in the hallway.

"Go home, Wakefield," Penny said. She stood and shut off her typewriter and desk lamp, then picked up her backpack. "Let your brain rest. Watch game shows. Play with something that comes in a cereal box. Listen to Jessica complain about her duties as Miss Teen Sweet Valley."

Elizabeth laughed, and it felt very good. Following Penny's lead, she turned off her own lamp and typewriter and gathered up her books. "I honestly think Jess would resign if she could stand to hand over her crown to the runner-up. But she's very attached to that crown!" Elizabeth said.

The two girls walked out of the building together and toward the lighted parking lot. "You heard about Tim Eastborne, I guess?"

Penny said when they were standing near their cars.

Elizabeth frowned. She had been preoccupied with her article almost all day, and had not paid much attention to the talk in the cafeteria or between classes in the halls. "No, what?"

"The police found Jerry's van and the guy who stole it. Tim was telling the truth when he said he was innocent."

"That's great," Elizabeth said delightedly. "About half the school owes him an apology."

Penny unlocked her car door and tossed her backpack inside. "Looks like nobody's going to get the *chance* to apologize. From what my source in the office tells me, Tim's checked out of Sweet Valley High, and his transcripts are being sent to some boarding school back East."

"That's too bad," Elizabeth said sadly. "I'll miss him."

Elizabeth got into the Fiat, Penny got into her own car, and they both drove away.

When she arrived at home Elizabeth found her father in the kitchen, making a warm chicken salad. A few days earlier she had talked to him, in confidence, about Tim Eastborne's problems.

"Tim won't be charged with stealing that van after all," she said as she put her things on the counter and helped herself to a cold drink from the refrigerator.

Mr. Wakefield smiled and nodded. "That's good."

"Penny said Tim's leaving Sweet Valley."

"*That's* too bad," Mr. Wakefield said. "From what you told me, Tim sounds like a good guy."

Just then Jessica dragged in, wearing furry slippers and a ratty old nightshirt.

"Are you sick?" Elizabeth asked.

"Just depressed," Jessica answered with a sigh melodramatic enough for the late show.

"Being a celebrity must have its drawbacks," Elizabeth said seriously.

Jessica narrowed her eyes at her twin, plopped an herbal-tea bag into a cup of water, and put it in the microwave. "That's not funny, Liz. If you think it's easy being *somebody*, you should just try it!"

Mr. Wakefield and Elizabeth looked at each other and laughed.

"I'll remember that sage observation, Jess," Elizabeth said. "If I should ever amount to anything, that is."

"You'd think I could get a little sympathy and understanding from my own family," Jessica whined. "But no. All anybody wants to do is pick on me!" She took her cup of tea from the microwave and left the room in an indignant huff.

A few minutes later, Elizabeth followed and knocked lightly at the door of her sister's room. Then, without waiting for an invitation, she walked in.

"What happened?" Elizabeth asked. She cleared off a space on the end of Jessica's rumpled bed so that she could sit.

"Dennis Hanover asked me to go surfing with him this weekend," Jessica answered tragically. "And I had to say no because of another *personal* appearance by Miss Teen Sweet Valley. Ugh!"

"Let's talk about it," Elizabeth said, trying to hide her smile.

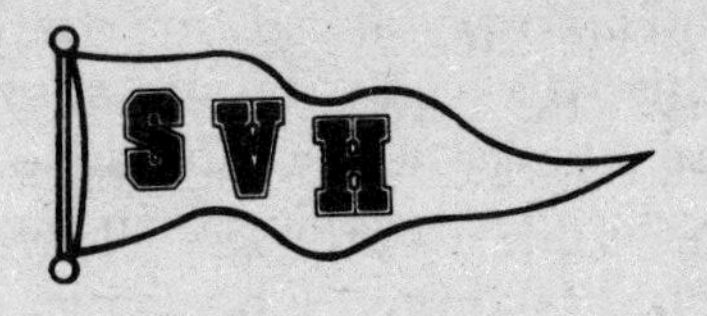

Ten

Thursday morning, Sara and Tim flipped a coin to see who would drive to school, and Tim won. When they pulled into the parking lot, Jerry McAllister was there again, leaning against his van. This time, none of his rowdy friends were in sight.

Sara set her jaw and got out of the car before Tim could tell her to stay put. Not that she would have listened to her brother—she was too angry.

Sara stomped right up to Jerry, too furious to be intimidated by his size and reputation, and demanded, "What do you want now, you big lug?"

A corner of Jerry's mouth quivered with amusement. Like Tim, he still had a few cuts and bruises from the fight. He looked past Sara to Tim.

"Call off your sister, Eastborne," he said. "I have something I want to say."

Gently, Tim took hold of Sara's shoulders and eased her aside.

"Which is?" he asked.

Jerry stuck out one hand and grinned. "Which is this," he said. "I'm sorry. I was wrong, thinking you'd taken my wheels just because of the rumors that were going around about you. And, well, when I heard that you and Amanda Hayes were spending a lot of time together, I guess I got jealous. See, I've kind of liked her for a while." He paused briefly, then added, "Buddies?"

Tim looked at Jerry's hand for a moment, then shook it. "Buddies," he said. But as soon as Jerry had pulled away in his van and he and Sara were headed for the school building again, Tim rolled his eyes.

"He actually apologized! I've never heard of Jerry doing that before," Sara exclaimed.

"Little wonder," Tim observed dryly. "I think he specializes in threats, as a general rule."

Sara laughed, light-headed with happiness and relief and the pure comedy of the idea of Tim and Jerry hanging out together. "He likes you. You're going to be *buddies*!"

"Not if I can help it," Tim grumbled as they entered the building.

Just about everyone at Sweet Valley High had already heard that Tim was transferring to a boarding school back East. His unexpected appearance in the hallway that morning started a commotion.

Todd Wilkins immediately came over and punched him playfully on the upper arm. "Hey, Tim! I thought you were history."

Tim shrugged as more kids, a large proportion of them female, clustered around. "I'm back," he said. "And I'm here to stay!"

Smiling to herself, Sara left her brother to his glory and went on to her locker. When she got there, Amanda was waiting for her.

Sara felt her spirits rise even further. "Hi, Amanda," she said. "Going to dance class tomorrow afternoon?"

Amanda looked at her and blushed. "Yeah, I thought I would," she said shyly. "How about you?"

Sara grinned. "The wrath of Mr. Krezenski is something I wouldn't want to risk," she said. "I'll be there."

"Maybe we could go together?"

The bell rang just then, and Sara and Amanda started to head to their first class. "I really am sorry I didn't trust you with the truth about Tim," Sara said as they walked through the crowded hall. "For what it's worth now, I had this friend, Darlene, in Connecticut, and after Tim got into trouble the first time, she—and most of the other kids in my school—wouldn't talk to me anymore. It may have been partly my fault."

"I've really missed you, Sara," Amanda said simply. "And I'm sorry for having been so stubborn and unreasonable."

Sara stopped and took Amanda's arm. "You know what?" she said. "You're my best friend ever."

At lunch, Sara and Amanda sat with Elizabeth and Enid.

"It's great to see you two hanging around together again," Elizabeth said.

"It's great to *be* hanging around together again," Sara answered.

"Jess and I just decided to throw a party Saturday night. You'll both come, won't you?"

"Sure," Sara and Amanda said in unison.

"Terrific," Elizabeth answered. "Bring your bathing suits." Just then, Todd and Tim joined the group at the table.

Sara noticed that Amanda's cheeks suddenly turned bright pink. Amanda muttered some excuse, picked up her tray, and fled the table.

"I sure know how to clear a room, don't I?" Tim laughed nervously. There was a sad look in his eyes as he watched Amanda return her tray and hurry out of the cafeteria.

Sara smiled at her brother reassuringly and rose to follow her friend. "Later, everybody," she said. She returned her tray and hurried after Amanda.

She found her friend in the bathroom, splashing cold water on her face.

"You really care about Tim, don't you?" Sara asked, grateful that the room wasn't crowded.

Amanda nodded. She dried her face with a paper towel and sniffled. "I blew it with him big time," she groaned, and when she tossed away the towel, Sara saw that her friend had been crying.

"You know," Sara said with a teasing grin, "that didn't do a whole lot for your makeup. You look like you were caught in a rainstorm."

In spite of her down mood, Amanda giggled. When she looked at herself in the mirror, though, she gasped and fumbled through her backpack for her makeup bag.

"I never thought I'd say this," Sara went on in a quiet and serious voice, "but my brother isn't the same person he was in Connecticut. He's different now, and you don't need to be afraid to like him."

Amanda lowered her eyeliner. "You think I'm afraid?"

"Yes," Sara answered softly. "I do. And I can't really blame you, because I was scared to trust Tim, too. But he's a really special guy, and you're going to be losing out if you don't give him a second chance."

"I do like him," Amanda confessed miserably. "I like him *so much.* Nobody has ever made me laugh the way he does."

"Well then?"

"I made a fool of myself," Amanda said. "But he's going to think I'm a fair-weather friend, that I ran away when he was in trouble and now that he's been cleared, I want to hang around together again."

"Listen to me. He's crazy about you," Sara said. "I'm going off to class now. I'll see you later, OK?"

Amanda smiled. "OK. And thanks, Sara."

Sara almost collided with Tim in the hallway outside the girls' bathroom.

"Is she all right?" he asked anxiously.

"I think she'll be fine," she assured him, touching his arm.

Sara headed out to the parking lot after school. She spotted Tim and Amanda strolling around the lot, probably waiting for her, but she was in no rush to join them. They looked pretty happy together, and Sara wanted to give them as much time alone as possible.

She was a little startled when Bob pulled up alongside her in his car and smiled as though he had never dumped her.

"Hi, Sara," he said. "Can I give you a lift?"

Although she still missed a part of their relationship, in the last twenty-four hours Sara had come to realize she didn't miss Bob himself. As far as she was concerned, Bob was a shallow creep. Amanda had at least had a *reason* to be angry: she had counted on Sara's trusting her and Sara had let her down. Bob, on the other hand, had simply been concerned with appearances.

"No, thanks," she said breezily. "I'll walk."

Bob cruised along beside her as she walked. "Sara, listen, the Wakefield twins are throwing a party Saturday night, and I'd like you to be my date. How about it?"

Sara stopped walking and turned to face Bob squarely. What had she ever seen in this arrogant jerk?

"I won't be needing a date," she said clearly and politely. "But thanks, anyway."

"Sara . . ."

Sara started to walk again. "You were correct before, Bob. We're just not right for each other. It won't work out."

Bob's tires screeched as he sped away, and the sound caught Tim and Amanda's attention. They turned, saw Sara walking behind them, and stopped to wait for her.

"What's that bozo's problem, anyway?" Tim demanded as he watched Bob's taillights disappear out of the lot.

"Who knows?" Sara shrugged. "In fact, who cares?"

On Saturday morning, Sara and Amanda met at the mall to buy new outfits to wear to Elizabeth and Jessica's party.

"Look," Amanda whispered. She giggled

and pointed toward the cheese shop. "Isn't that Jessica Wakefield?"

Sara followed the direction of Amanda's finger and saw the dazzling sparkle of a rhinestone tiara, the elegant drape of a satin sash, and a blue-green formal that looked like something out of a fairy tale.

"I think so," she whispered. "But if it *is* Jessica, there's something different about her." Sara noted a certain serenity in the girl's smile, though it was obvious, even from a distance, that the last thing Miss Teen Sweet Valley wanted to be doing was passing out cheese samples in the mall.

"C'mon," Amanda said. "Let's go find out."

Amanda and Sara approached the cheese shop.

"Hi, Jessica," Amanda said.

Miss Teen Sweet Valley winked. "If you say so," she replied brightly.

"*Elizabeth?* Is that you?" Sara asked.

A twinkle in the girl's aquamarine eyes confirmed Sara's suspicion. "Of course not," Elizabeth said, smiling and showing her dimple, which, like the rest of her features, was an exact duplicate of Jessica's. "Elizabeth wouldn't think of putting on a tiara and sash and parading around the Valley Mall. She has her reputation as a feminist and a newspaperwoman to consider, you know."

Sara laughed, delighted by the masquerade. "How did Jessica get you to do this?"

Elizabeth looked at Sara innocently. "Whatever are you talking about?" she whispered as she turned back to her job of forcing cheese samples on passers-by.

"*Was* that Jessica or wasn't it?" Amanda demanded as they walked away.

Sara grinned. "I'll never tell," she said. "As a twin myself, I'm bound to secrecy!" The girls walked into their favorite boutique. "So, I've been meaning to ask you, though I didn't want to pry—did you and Tim really make up? Or have you decided to be just friends?"

Amanda blushed. "He's my date for the party tonight," she said.

"No kidding? That's great!"

"What about you?" Amanda asked as she examined the skirt of a pink summer dress. "Do you have a date?"

"No," Sara answered forthrightly. "Bob asked me, but I turned him down."

"Which was why he left half an inch of rubber pulling out of the parking lot the other day," Amanda observed.

"Something like that." Sara smiled as she took a sleek jumpsuit from the rack and held it up in front of her.

"You know," Amanda said, "I never did like Bob Hillman very much."

"Why didn't you ever tell me?" Sara asked.

Amanda shrugged. "I was afraid of hurting your feelings. I guess I'm also guilty of not trusting my best friend."

"And you're forgiven!"

"You know, Sara, it used to really bother you, the idea of not having a date for every party," Amanda said cautiously.

Sara put the jumpsuit back on the rack and reached for another outfit. "I know," she admitted. "But I've decided to work on getting to know and like *myself* a little more before I try to know and like a guy. Does that make any sense?"

Her friend smiled. "It makes a *lot* of sense, Sara," she said. "And you know what? You're going to find out that you're one super person."

"You're prejudiced," Sara accused.

Amanda shrugged, inspected the price tag on a silky white pants outfit, and flinched. "Mom and Dad would have to take out a second mortgage to pay for this."

"You owe me, Jessica Wakefield," Elizabeth said as she tossed the tiara and sash onto Jessica's bed with a sigh of relief. "You owe me *big*."

Jessica was sitting in front of her bureau lining her lips with a pink pencil, her face about an inch and a half from her makeup mirror. "Come on, Liz. How hard could it have been to pass out a few chunks of cheese?"

Elizabeth began to unhook the little clasps at the back of the formal. "It was terrible. My feet are sore from standing there in those stupid high heels, and three women came up to me at three different times to tell me that beauty pageants are silly and destructive. Do you know how hard it was to keep smiling and passing out Gouda and cheddar and Monterey Jack, and pretending I *liked* it?"

Jessica gave a saintly sigh. "Now you understand, Elizabeth. My life is *not* an easy one."

Elizabeth let out a strangled cry of sheer frustration, and fell backward onto her sister's bed.

"Get up, Liz," Jessica said as she turned back to the mirror. "You're going to get my formal all wrinkled."

"Well, excuuuuuuuuse me! Imagine my having the nerve to die on your formal!"

Jessica shook her head. "Sometimes I wonder about you, Elizabeth Wakefield," she said solemnly. "Sometimes I really wonder about you."

Elizabeth rolled her eyes and then wriggled out of the formal. Their party was scheduled to start in less than an hour, and she still had to shower and get dressed.

"Liz?"

Elizabeth stopped in the doorway to the bathroom between their two rooms. "Yes?"

Jessica treated her to a dazzling, Miss Teen Sweet Valley smile. "Thanks for helping me out."

* * *

Colorful Chinese lanterns had been strung up around the Wakefield's backyard, and there was enough food spread out on various tables to satisfy the entire high school.

Feeling confident in her new black shorts and red scoop-neck top, Sara looked around until she spotted Elizabeth. At least, she *thought* it was Elizabeth.

"Liz?" she asked.

Elizabeth winked, just as she had earlier that day at the mall. Her mischievous smile showed her famous dimple. "Did she or didn't she? Only her twin knows for sure. Speaking of twins, it looks like your brother has managed to iron out his differences with Amanda."

Sara followed Elizabeth's gaze and saw Tim and Amanda dancing close. "They look like they're going to fall into each other's eyes," Sara said with a sigh.

"Yes," Elizabeth agreed. "Isn't it romantic?"

"Yeah. And this is a great party, Elizabeth," she said sincerely. "Did you do all this decorating yourself?"

"Mom did it," Elizabeth confided. "I was, uh, busy, and Jessica had a big date this afternoon. By the way, did you come to the party by yourself?"

"*With* myself," Sara corrected her friend.

Elizabeth grinned. "Here's to good company." She raised her glass of soda in an enthusiastic toast. Then she took Sara's arm. "Come on. I want to introduce you to some of my brother's friends."

Sara had a great time at Elizabeth and Jessica's party. She danced until she was breathless, and when everybody decided to swim, she changed into her suit and plunged in. When Michael Harris and his girlfriend, April Dawson, drove Sara home late that night, Sara found her mother in the kitchen, dressed in her quilted robe and brewing herbal tea.

"Did you get the big account?" Sara asked, even though she knew by the happy look in Mrs. Eastborne's eyes that she had accomplished everything she had set out to do.

"Sure did. Where's Tim?"

"He'll be home in a little while," Sara answered. "He and Amanda have a lot to talk about."

Mrs. Eastborne smiled. "Do you know how glad I am to have both my children living in the same house again? This time is precious to me, you know. Before long, you'll probably be in L.A. going to college and Tim will be in vocational school. I'll be a lonely old lady, rattling around in this big house all by myself."

Sara laughed and pretended to play a violin. "What you need," Sara said resolutely, "is a guy."

"Maybe I'm finally ready for that," Mrs. Eastborne replied softly.

"Is there somebody?" Sara asked anxiously.

Mrs. Eastborne shrugged, and her eyes took on a mischievous twinkle. "How would you feel if there was?"

"I don't know," Sara confessed. "Is he nice?

What's his name? When do Tim and I get to check this guy out?"

Her mother laughed. "Yes, he's nice, and his name is Frank Williams. He's an executive with the company we'll be designing the new shopping complex for. As for when you and Tim can meet him, well, I've invited him to come for dinner next Friday night."

Sara let out a shriek of pure glee and flung her arms around her mother. "It's about *time!*" she cried. "Does he live here in Sweet Valley?"

Mrs. Eastborne shook her head. "No, he has a house in L.A. But he's got his own helicopter, and he can drop in any time he wants to."

"Wow! He sounds like James Bond!"

"Who sounds like James Bond?" Tim asked as he came in to the kitchen. Sara noticed a smudge of Amanda's apricot lipstick on his chin.

Mrs. Eastborne hugged her son. "Sit down," she said, gesturing toward the table, "and I'll tell you all about him."

Sara smiled. It was so good to have home *feel* like home again.

April Dawson smiled up at Mike Harris as he walked into her father's garage, where she was working on her dirt bike. There was a lot to do before the big race in a few weeks, and April wanted to be ready.

"You look great, even with grease on your face," Mike said, with a grin that made April's heart slip into a higher gear.

"Thanks," April said. "If that was a compliment, I mean."

Mike laughed. "Believe me, it was," he said. "Come on, let's get this bike in shape. I've got my dad's pickup truck today. We can go out and ride our bikes on the beach."

"Great." April stood up and wiped her hands on her jeans.

Michael walked around April's bike, inspecting it carefully. "You know," he said, "I was thinking this morning about Jerry McAllister's van being stolen. I think Crunch was a jerk for accusing Tim Eastborne without having any proof, but I can really understand how upset he must have been. I mean, if anyone stole my bike, or if anyone did anything to sabotage me and my racing, I'd really freak out."

April saw that Michael's face had turned beet red and that his fists were clenched at his sides. She had seen him like this before, suddenly angry and looking as if he could tear down a wall. The strange thing was, it only seemed to happen whenever he talked about his bike. Which was often, particularly before an important race.

"Hey, Mike," April said. She went over to him and took his arm. "Take it easy. Your bike is safe and sound. And no one's trying to sabotage your racing career. And if someone *were*, I'd take care of him!"

Michael gave a short laugh and turned away from her. "Oh, yeah? Where were you when I needed you?"

April stepped back and looked at him curiously. "What do you mean? Did something happen before we started going out? Is that why you get so tense all the time right before a race?"

When Michael didn't answer right away, April pressed on. "Hey, it didn't have anything to do with Artie Western, did it? I've noticed that whenever we see him at a race you start acting really odd—"

"Nothing happened," Michael interrupted. "I was only kidding before. And do me a favor, will you? Don't bring up the subject of Western anymore, OK?"

"OK. Fine. I won't say another word about it," April promised. But in spite of Michael's denial, April knew she had gotten closer to the truth that morning than she ever had. Something bad had happened to Michael before she knew him, and it had involved Artie Western. *I'm going to find out what that something was,* she decided.

What secret is Michael keeping from April? Find out in Sweet Valley High #80, **THE GIRL THEY BOTH LOVED.**